THE MELANIE BROWN STORIES

The
MELANIE BROWN
Stories

PAMELA OLDFIELD

Illustrated by
CAROLYN DINAN

faber and faber

LONDON · BOSTON

This paperback edition first published in 1994
by Faber and Faber Limited
3 Queen Square London WC1N 3AU

The stories in Part One were first published in
Melanie Brown Goes to School, 1970
The stories in Part Two were first published in
Melanie Brown Climbs a Tree, 1972
The stories in Part Three were first published in
Melanie Brown and the Jar of Sweets, 1974
by Faber and Faber Limited

Printed in England by Clays Ltd, St Ives plc

A CIP record for this book is
available from the British Library.

ISBN 0-571-17064-1

2 4 6 8 10 9 7 5 3 1

Contents

PART THREE

PART ONE

for
CAROLE and DAVID

Melanie Brown and the Box of Straws

Melanie Brown had brown hair, and she wore it in two bunches. She was a naughty little girl, and she always had her own way. So when she reached the age of five and decided to go to school, that was that.

Her mother bought her a grey pleated skirt, a white blouse and a red jumper. There was also a grey blazer to wear over it. Melanie Brown put it all on and decided that it suited her, so that was no problem.

Grandmother gave her a new brown satchel, and on the 7th of September Melanie Brown went to school. She had quite made up her mind to like it, so she did.

She liked her teacher, whose name was Miss Bradley. She liked the big sunny classroom with the tables and chairs that were just the right size. She liked the sand-tray with the rubber buckets and spades. Also the Wendy House with the dolls and the cot and the pretend stove with its saucepans and kettle. She liked the big building bricks, the paints and crayons, the plasticine and the beads and many other things.

Then there were the stories. Miss Bradley was good at telling stories. She told the children stories about animals, stories about magic, stories about trains and buses, stories about children. There were sad stories

I

and funny stories and stories about real things that happen in the world.

But although Melanie Brown enjoyed all these things there was one thing that she longed to do, and that was to give out the straws at milk-time. Every morning two boys from another class came in with a crateful of milk bottles. The teacher made a hole in each silver milk top and chose one child to give out the bottles, and another to give out the straws. Melanie Brown watched very carefully, and it looked quite simple.

So one morning, as soon as the big boys came in with the milk, she held her hand right up in the air, so that the teacher was sure to notice it.

'What is it, Melanie?' asked the teacher.

'Please, Miss Bradley, may I give out the straws?'

Miss Bradley looked at her doubtfully. Melanie Brown had only been at school for a few days.

'I think not today,' she said, 'but you may clean the blackboard if you like.'

Melanie Brown stared at her in amazement.

'Oh, but, Miss Bradley – I don't want to clean the blackboard,' she said firmly. 'I only want to give out the straws, because I'm *good* at giving out straws, but I'm *not* good at cleaning blackboards.'

Miss Bradley laughed.

'Oh, well. You can try, I suppose. Fetch the straws from the cupboard.'

Feeling very important, Melanie Brown went to the big cupboard where the straws were kept. She hoped that all the children were watching her. A boy called Jimmy was giving out the bottles.

Standing on tiptoe she took down the box and began to walk round. She looked in the box. Melanie Brown had never seen so many straws. She could not see all of each straw because they were standing up on end, packed closely together, but she could see the top of each one, like a tiny round hole. Suddenly she decided to count them.

'One, two, four, seven – ' she began, but she was not very good at counting.

She started again. 'One, two, three, seven, five, eight – ' No, that was not right.

Carefully, Melanie Brown began again, touching each straw as she said a number.

'One, two, three, eleven, eight, twenty – ' She was so busy counting that she had forgotten what she was supposed to be doing. The children watched her impatiently.

'Melanie, hurry up, dear,' said Miss Bradley. 'Christopher's table is waiting for straws.'

Melanie Brown frowned, and looked up.

'I'm trying to count them,' she said crossly, 'but the numbers keep going wrong.'

'Well, you must finish giving them out now, or else let Jennifer do it. It's nearly playtime.'

Melanie Brown suddenly remembered that she had meant to show everyone how quickly she could do the job. She darted forward towards Christopher's table, caught her elbow against the corner of Miss Bradley's desk and dropped the box. As it fell, the straws scat-

3

tered in all directions. Melanie Brown stared at them, where they lay, all white and new-looking. She thought there must be hundreds and hundreds of them. Or millions and millions.

The silence that followed was broken by Jennifer.

'Miss Bradley, Melanie Brown's dropped the straws!'

Melanie Brown looked slowly up at the teacher's face. She felt so terrible that she almost decided to give up school altogether.

But Miss Bradley only sighed.

'Never mind, Melanie, it was an accident. Perhaps Jennifer will help you to pick them up. We'll put them back in the box and use them for something else.'

And she sent Christopher into the next class for another box of straws and told him to finish giving them out. Melanie Brown was rather disappointed about that but Christopher was a very nice boy and he put two straws in her bottle, instead of only one. She looked at him carefully. He had fair hair and big blue eyes and such a nice smile that Melanie Brown decided to marry him when she grew up.

That afternoon Miss Bradley showed the children how to make shapes using the straws and some pipe-cleaners. She bent a pipe-cleaner in the middle and slipped a straw on to each half. That made a corner. Then she bent two more pipe-cleaners and fitted them into the straws. One more straw and it turned into a triangle. Then the children made some shapes. Melanie Brown made a square and Christopher made a shape with five sides, called a pentagon.

Melanie Brown thought he was the cleverest boy in the class. She was almost glad then that she had been chosen to give out the straws.

Melanie Brown and the Pencil Sharpener

Melanie Brown liked school. She liked it the very first day, and every day she liked it a little bit more. She liked going into the hall, which was a big room with no desks in it. There was a piano at one end, and a stage at the other. Sometimes they went into the hall for singing and games, and Miss Bradley played the piano. They also went into the hall for prayers, with all the other classes.

Melanie Brown enjoyed it all so much that when Saturday came, and there was no school she was very disappointed. She was especially disappointed because she wanted to sharpen the pencils. The child who did that job was allowed to go into school early, so that the pencils would be ready for the others when they came in. Melanie Brown was quite sure that she would be good at sharpening pencils.

The reason was simple. Miss Bradley had a special pencil sharpener. It was made of shiny green metal, but you could look through a tiny plastic window to see what was happening inside. To sharpen a pencil you put it into a hole at one side of the sharpener, and turned a handle on the other side. Little shavings of wood came off the pencil and made the point sharp again.

Melanie Brown made up her mind to ask Miss Bradley if she could have the job on Monday, and she could hardly wait. But on Monday it was raining hard, and she wore her new black wellingtons and her mackintosh with the hood. The boots were made of rubber so Melanie Brown thought they ought to be bouncy, so she jumped over a puddle to see if they were. They were, so she tried to jump over a large puddle, but she landed right in the middle of it, and sat down with a great splash. When she got up again she was so wet she had to go home and change her clothes.

By the time she reached school the pencils were already sharpened. She was so disappointed that she could not do her work properly, and did some rather horrible writing patterns in her book. Miss Bradley gave red stars to the children who had tried hard, but she frowned at Melanie Brown's book, and did not give her a star.

Melanie Brown was surprised at how badly the day was going, but suddenly she had an idea. Miss Bradley had a special red pencil for marking the books. She would sharpen it and give Miss Bradley a surprise! She waited patiently until playtime, and went out into the playground with the other children. When Miss Bradley left the classroom to have her coffee, Melanie Brown went up to the teacher who was looking after them in the playground.

'Please, Mrs Jones,' she said, 'may I go into the classroom to fetch my hanky?'

It was rather naughty of her, because the hanky was in her pocket all the time.

Mrs Jones said 'Yes,' so she hurried inside. It was quiet in the classroom with all the children outside. She went straight to Miss Bradley's desk and looked for the red pencil. It was not on the desk, so she opened the drawer and there it was, next to the pen. It was a new pencil, very long, with gold writing along one side. Quickly she put it into the pencil sharpener, and began to turn the handle.

It made a lovely grinding noise. When she looked in through the plastic window, she saw little curly pieces of wood being shaved off the pencil. She began to turn the handle faster and faster, in case playtime ended before she had finished. As the handle went round the sound reminded her of a train going along. She slowed the handle down, to let the train stop at the station, then speeded it up again as it went on its journey.

When at last she took the pencil out it had a very sharp point, but it looked much smaller than before. Melanie Brown pressed it into the desk, and it made a tiny hole, but then the point snapped right off, so she had to start all over again. She looked through the plastic window, but there were so many curls of wood she could not see the pencil point. With a last burst of energy she sent the handle whizzing round. When her arm began to ache she stopped and drew out the pencil. She looked at it carefully. It was very short. So short, in fact, that all the gold writing had disappeared, and that made her wonder if something had gone wrong.

At that moment the whistle blew and playtime was over. Melanie Brown put the pencil back into the desk and ran outside to line up with the others. Nothing happened for a long time after that. Miss Bradley told them a story about Jack and the Beanstalk. Then they drew a picture about it, while one of the older girls read her reading book to Miss Bradley.

Then Miss Bradley looked in her desk for her long red pencil. When she found it she looked very puzzled indeed.

'Who has been playing about with my pencil?' she asked.

Most of the children looked up at her in surprise, but Melanie Brown went on drawing.

'Melanie Brown, have you done this?' said Miss Bradley, holding up the pencil. Everyone stared when they saw how small it was.

'Please, Miss Bradley, I wanted to sharpen it, and give you a surprise,' said Melanie Brown, in a voice that was almost as small as the pencil.

'Well, you have certainly given me a surprise, but not a very nice one,' said Miss Bradley. 'When did you do it?'

When Melanie Brown told her she was rather cross at first, but then she began to smile, and every time she looked at the pencil she smiled a bit more. Then, of course, all the children began to laugh – even Melanie Brown.

Miss Bradley said that luckily she had another red pencil, so they could all get on with their work, but she asked Melanie Brown not to give her any more surprises, and Melanie Brown said she would try.

Melanie Brown Cuts Out

Melanie Brown had brown hair, tied with ribbon in two bunches, one at each side of her head. When it was not tied in bunches, it hung down almost to her shoulders. She had always liked the bunches but not any more. Because Pat had long fair hair that hung down to her waist in twisty curls called ringlets. And that is what Melanie Brown wanted, only her ringlets would have to be brown.

So the next time Mrs Brown wanted to take her to the hairdresser, to have her hair trimmed, she made such a fuss that finally Mrs Brown said she could grow it. Every day Pat measured it for her with a tape-measure, and it was growing very nicely when something unfortunate happened.

One day Melanie Brown came in from the playground and found scissors and coloured paper on the desks. Miss Bradley showed the children how to fold the paper and make little snips round it. When she unfolded the paper, they were surprised to see that the holes had made a pattern. They all hurried back to their desks and started to make patterns of their own. Now Melanie Brown was not very good at cutting out. She made the snips too big and then cut the

paper in half by mistake. She tried again, but then the snips were too small, and when she unfolded the paper there was hardly any pattern.

But John's pattern was very good, and he pasted it on to a sheet of white paper. The white paper showed through the holes and looked very attractive. Pat's pattern was good, too, and she pasted hers on to black paper. Melanie Brown looked at her scissors to see what was the matter with them, but they looked just like all the other scissors. Miss Bradley gave her another piece of paper, and helped her to make a few snips. Then she tried again on her own, but when she opened it out all the snips had joined together into one big hole. Scowling, Melanie Brown screwed it up and dropped it on the floor under her desk. At once John put his hand up.

'Miss Bradley, Melanie Brown has thrown hers on the floor.'

But Miss Bradley did not hear him. Melanie Brown took Pat's scissors while she was not looking. John put his hand up again.

'Miss Bradley, Melanie Brown has taken Pat's scissors.'

Miss Bradley hurried over to them.

'All the scissors are the same,' she said. 'If you don't want to make a pattern, Melanie, why not make a picture instead – a house or a clown, perhaps.'

Pat leaned over the table.

'Shall I help you to make a pattern?' she asked kindly.

Melanie Brown's scowl deepened.

'I don't want to make a pattern,' she said, 'because I don't even like patterns. I'm going to make a house.'

She cut out a square for the house and a triangle for the roof. But the roof was too small for the top of the house, so she cut out a much bigger roof and pasted it on over the small one.

'Look at my house,' she said, in a pleased voice. John looked at it.

'It hasn't got any windows or any door.'

'I'm just going to make them,' said Melanie Brown crossly, and she cut out a little red door and four blue windows. When John saw it he liked it so much he decided to make a house, too. But Pat did not like it at all.

'The windows are bigger than the door,' she said, 'and the roof is too big.'

Angrily Melanie Brown poked her tongue out at her, and Pat pulled a horrible face back. Melanie Brown turned to John.

'I don't like houses,' she said in a loud voice. 'I'm going to make a clown.'

But even the clown went wrong, and then it was time to stop. Melanie Brown put her hand up at once.

'Please can I collect the scissors, Miss Bradley?'

'No, I'm afraid not, Melanie, it's Stephen's turn today.'

Melanie Brown sat back in her chair, swung her legs, and hated everything! She hated school; she hated cutting out; she hated Pat and John; and most of all she hated Stephen. She hated Stephen so much that when he came to collect her scissors she hid them in her desk, and pretended they were lost. There was no time to look for them because they had to go into the hall to watch a programme on the television. Melanie Brown did not enjoy it very much, because Pat was not her friend any more, and they did not sit together as they usually did.

When they went back to the classroom Miss Bradley chose six patterns to put up on the wall. One of them was Pat's and that made Melanie Brown so jealous she wanted to do something really bad to her. She took the scissors out of her desk, and cut the end off one of Pat's ringlets! Pat turned round quickly and saw the little curl on the floor. She snatched the scissors and made a big snip in Melanie Brown's hair. Melanie

Brown screamed, and tried to get the scissors back again, and then John joined in. They made such a noise Miss Bradley heard them.

She took the scissors away at once, and was very cross with both the girls. But when she found out just how naughty Melanie Brown had been she sent her to sit at an empty desk all by herself. She also wrote a note to each girl's mother to explain what had happened.

When Mrs Brown saw Melanie Brown's hair she said it would have to be trimmed, because one side was so much shorter than the other. Melanie Brown cried and cried when she heard that, but when she looked in the mirror she saw just how funny it looked, and started to laugh.

'Anyway,' she said defiantly. 'I don't like long hair any more,' and she blew her nose very loudly, and that was that!

Melanie Brown and the Dinner-Money

Monday was dinner-money day. A few of the children went home to dinner, but most of them had their dinner at school, in the big hall. So every Monday they took their dinner-money to school and Miss Bradley collected it. Some children, like Melanie Brown, took their money in a purse so that they would not lose it on the way to school. Some took it in an envelope, but one or two of them carried it in their hands.

One of these children was called Jimmy, and one Monday, while he was taking off his coat, he dropped his money on the floor. All the children were taking off their hats and coats and changing their shoes, so it was very difficult to see where the money went to. Jimmy searched for a few minutes and found what he could. Then he sat down in his place.

'Children with dinner-money come out, please,' said Miss Bradley, and she counted the money from each child and wrote it down in the dinner book. When it was Jimmy's turn she said, 'I think you've lost some of yours, Jimmy.' So he told her what had happened.

'You'd better have another look for it,' she said. 'Take someone to help you.'

So Jimmy chose Melanie Brown and together they

searched the cloakroom. They looked along the window-sill, under the shoe baskets, and even under the doormat, but it was no good. They could not find the missing money.

Then Jimmy said he might have dropped some of it in the playground before he came into school, so Miss Bradley sent them outside to look. They found a blue glove belonging to a girl in the top class, and took it in to her. They asked the top class if anyone had found any money, but no one had. Jimmy looked very miserable.

'My mother will be cross with me,' he said, 'when she knows I've lost my money.'

Melanie Brown felt sorry for him.

'Maybe you dropped it in the lane coming to school,' she suggested. 'Let's ask Miss Bradley if we can look in the lane.'

When they got back into the classroom it was time to go into the hall for prayers, but Miss Bradley said they could go afterwards.

All the other classes were in the hall with their teachers. Mrs Jones played some quiet music on the piano until the headmistress came in. Then they all said 'Good morning,' and sang a hymn called 'All things bright and beautiful' which was Melanie Brown's favourite. She did not know all the words, but she liked to hum the tune and listen to the older children. Then they put their hands together to help them think, and said a prayer about animals, and another one about people who were ill.

When they got back to the classroom Miss Bradley said they could go and look in the lane.

'But only for five minutes,' she told them, 'because it is nearly time for singing.'

The two children promised to be very quick, and off they went.

It was strange to be the only children out of school. It was quiet in the lane. Melanie Brown glanced back at the school. Denise and Christopher were watching them out of the window so she waved to them. Then she climbed up into the hedge and jumped down again, just for the fun of it. Jimmy tried it too, and they had a game to see who could jump the furthest. But then Jimmy slipped down and made his trousers all muddy, so they stopped that game and started to look for the money.

There was a field on one side of the lane, with a pond in it. The children collected ten stones each and they tossed them over the hedge into the pond, where they fell with a nice 'plopping' sound.

Then Jimmy found a small frog and tried to catch it, but the frog was a very good jumper, and at last he gave up in disgust.

'I like toads best,' he told Melanie Brown, 'because they don't keep jumping about all the time. Frogs are silly, aren't they?'

She agreed. Actually, she did not like toads or frogs, but she did not want to say so. By that time they had reached Mr Bloggs's cottage at the end of the lane. Mr Bloggs was the school caretaker. His fluffy black cat was sitting on the door-step in the sunshine, so they stroked it for a while. They tried to teach it to beg, but it was not very interested, and kept closing its eyes.

Then, with a rattle and a clatter, the milk van turned the corner into the lane. The children ran up to the milkman, both talking at once. He was surprised to see them there.

'Well, and what are you two up to?' he said.

They told him about the lost dinner-money.

'I'm afraid I can't help you there,' he said, 'but if you've finished looking for it, I'll take you back to school in the van.'

Eagerly they scrambled up into the front of the van and squashed up together on the small leather seat. It was a marvellous ride! The milkman whistled happily, the engine whirred, and the bottles shook and clinked together whenever they went over a bump in the road. It was all over much too soon. Melanie Brown wanted to make the adventure last a little longer, so she asked the milkman if they could help him to unload the bottles for the school.

'Well,' he said, 'I suppose you could. I'll do the big crates, and you can get the big bottles for the school kitchen.'

So they carried the big bottles from the van to the kitchen door, but just as Melanie Brown was carrying the last one, the milkman said, 'Oh, dear, here comes your headmistress.'

Melanie Brown took one look at the headmistress's face, and dropped the bottle. It smashed on the ground, and the milk spread out in a big white pool. 'What on earth are you two doing out here?' asked the headmistress. 'And who dropped that bottle?'

Just as the milkman was trying to explain Miss Bradley came out and *she* started to explain. The two children wisely said nothing at all, but when the explaining was over, they were in disgrace.

'I told you not to be more than five minutes,' Miss Bradley reminded them. 'You have missed the singing lesson.'

'But we were only looking for the dinner-money,' Jimmy protested, rather untruthfully.

'Susan found the money soon after you had gone,' said Miss Bradley, 'it was in her shoe. You have been naughty children and you will stay in at playtime.'

Jimmy was sorry, then, because he wanted to play football with his big brother at playtime. But not

22

Melanie Brown. She was not a bit sorry. It had been such a marvellous adventure – she thought it was well worth it!

Melanie Brown and the Cress

One morning Miss Bradley told them some exciting news. They were going to grow something in the class-room! Melanie Brown was very surprised, because there was no earth in the classroom. But Miss Bradley was talking about cress seeds. She showed them the picture on the seed packet, so that they would know what they were growing. When the cress had grown they could cut it and eat it.

'I'll bring some biscuits and butter,' she said, 'and it will be just like a picnic.'

They covered two large plates with white lint, and wetted it under the tap.

'Now,' said Miss Bradley, 'I'll give you each some seeds in your hand, and you can sprinkle them on to the plates. Try not to blow or cough on to the seeds, or they will be blown away.'

Melanie Brown waited breathlessly for her turn. The little brown seeds trickled out of the packet, into her outstretched hand. It felt so tickly she laughed. Yes, she laughed all over them, and away they flew. She stared at her empty hand. Miss Bradley sighed.

'Never mind, I'll give you some more.'

And out they trickled again, into her hand, and she

did *not* laugh. She carried them carefully to the plates, and let them fall on to the wet lint. Soon both plates were covered with a layer of tiny brown seeds.

'Now,' said Miss Bradley, 'we must take care of them. We'll leave them on the window-sill in the sunshine, and we'll water them every day, so they won't dry up.'

And they did. They took it in turns to water them, and every morning they hurried in to see how much the cress had grown overnight. But one day something went wrong with the cress, and this is how it happened. Melanie Brown was playing in the Wendy House, with Stephen, Denise, and Christopher. A Wendy House is a big play house, with a door that really opens and a window you can look through. Melanie Brown and Christopher were Mother and Father. Denise was the baby, and Stephen was the doctor. It was a good game. They dressed up in clothes from the dressing-up box, and the baby pretended to be ill.

The doctor looked at the baby's throat.

'The baby's got the measles,' he said. 'I'll go and get some special stuff to make her better.'

And he went out through the little door, to look for some pretend medicine. He saw the cress, and without stopping to think he pulled up a few stalks. When he gave them to the baby she was surprised, but she ate it all up. When the mother saw the baby eating the cress, she suddenly felt an attack of measles coming on. So did the father. The poor doctor had to fetch more and more cress.

Finally, of course, one plate of cress was empty, so they had to start on the other one. Then the doctor got the measles and he had to have some. All this time, Miss Bradley was busy with another group of children. She noticed how quietly the children were playing in the Wendy House, and she was pleased, because sometimes they argued about who was going to cook the dinner, and other important things.

When it was time to stop, the children put away the dressing-up clothes, and forgot about the game. But that afternoon Miss Bradley took some butter from her bag, and a packet of biscuits, so the children guessed what was going to happen. Miss Bradley chose three of them to butter the biscuits, and they all grew more and more excited. But the four naughty children grew more and more worried. They looked at each other and wondered what would happen when Miss Bradley found the empty plates.

Higher and higher grew the pile of buttered biscuits until at last they were all done. It was time to start the picnic! Miss Bradley sent Nicholas to fetch the cress, but all he found were the empty plates.

'It's gone,' he said, in a shocked voice. Everyone stared at him in astonishment. He showed them the two empty plates. Then Miss Bradley was really upset. She had planned such a lovely treat for them, and now it was spoilt. The children were so disappointed, they looked at each other in silent dismay.

'Someone very naughty has done this,' she said, 'and I want to know who it is.'

There was no answer. She looked slowly round the class. Suddenly Denise stood up, holding her tummy.

'Please, Miss Bradley, I feel sick,' she said.

Then Stephen stood up, too.

'I feel sick,' he said, and Miss Bradley looked at them in surprise. Reluctantly, Christopher stood up, and then Melanie Brown. Looking at their faces, Miss Bradley suddenly guessed *why* they were feeling sick.

'You four had better come out and tell me all about it,' she said.

They told her about the measles and the medicine, and as they did so, they began to realize how greedy and unkind it was, to leave nothing for the other children.

'You must tell the children how sorry you are,' said Miss Bradley. So they did.

'And I don't think you had better play in the Wendy House any more this week, because you might do something else naughty.'

The rest of the class ate the nice buttered biscuits, but there were none for the four naughty ones. Miss Bradley said they would grow some more cress another day, but somehow Melanie Brown was not very interested. She had had enough cress to last her for a long, long time!

Melanie Brown and the Green Shorts

Twice a week the children had a turn on the big apparatus. It was all set up in the hall for them and it was great fun. There were ladders and ropes, and a rope ladder. There were planks to slide down, and bars to swing on. All the children loved the big apparatus. Whenever they went on the big apparatus they wore shorts and T-shirts. Miss Bradley told them why.

'Your ordinary clothes would get in the way when you are climbing, and you might trip and fall. You would soon get too hot, too. Shorts and shirts are much more sensible.'

Melanie Brown understood this, but she did not like wearing hers. The reason was this. She was very vain, and she did not think they suited her. The shirt was white, but the shorts were green. Melanie Brown did not like green. One day she spoke to Miss Bradley about it.

'Please could I have some different shorts, because green doesn't suit me. Have you got any red ones?'

But Miss Bradley only laughed at the idea. 'Don't be silly, Melanie,' she said. 'Everyone else wears green without any fuss. The colour doesn't matter at all.'

But Melanie Brown thought differently, and

decided to do something about it. She would hide the shorts and pretend they were lost. But where could she hide them? There was nowhere in the classroom, but the door into the playground was open and that gave her an idea. Quickly she took her shorts and slipped outside. She looked around, and saw – a drain-pipe. Without wasting a moment she pushed her shorts up into the pipe. When she was satisfied that they were out of sight she ran back into school, feeling very pleased with herself.

When it was time to change for the big apparatus Melanie Brown pretended to look for her shorts.

'Oh, Miss Bradley,' she said, in a surprised voice, 'I can't find my shorts.'

Miss Bradley had a look around.

'That's funny,' she said. 'Has anyone put Melanie's shorts on by mistake?'

Nobody had. She had another look, but of course she did not find them.

'Well, you can wear your knickers and vest just for today, Melanie.'

But Melanie Brown would *not*.

'Shall I ask my mother to buy me some red shorts?' she asked hopefully.

'Certainly not. We shall find them, sooner or later. Now if you won't wear your knickers and vest, you will have to sit and watch.'

So she did, and it was very boring. Christopher called out to her.

'Look at me – I'm upside down.'

Melanie Brown pulled a face at him, and would not

watch. Jennifer was hanging sideways on the bar, and Miss Bradley said she was a clever girl. Melanie Brown snorted loudly. 'Anyone can do that, it's easy,' she said. Nobody took any notice, however. They were enjoying themselves too much.

She sat and sulked until the lesson was over. Then Miss Bradley told them the story of Cinderella, and that made her forget all about the green shorts.

Later, while they were eating their dinner, it started to rain. Not just a shower, but a real downpour.

'It's a cloudburst,' said Christopher.

'I think it's a tropical storm,' said Nicholas, who had seen a tropical storm on the television.

They watched with interest as the rain lashed down. In no time at all the playground was full of big puddles. Suddenly, a lot of water began to overflow from the gutter. It poured down the window in a great sheet of water. The headmistress jumped up from the table.

'The gutter must be blocked,' she said. 'I'd better send for Mr Bloggs.'

Mr Bloggs, the caretaker, was a small, neat man. He always wore a dark blue boiler-suit. The children all believed he even went to bed in it. He arrived just as they were eating their apple pie. He was in a very bad mood. 'Messing about in all this rain – it's enough to give me my death of cold,' he grumbled. But he went off to the shed and came back with the ladder.

As soon as the children had finished their dinners, they hurried into the classroom to watch Mr Bloggs. He went up the ladder, carrying a long stick, in case he found what was blocking the gutter. Then he came down again, moved the ladder along a few yards, and went up again. He got wetter and wetter and his temper got worse and worse. But he found nothing. One of the big boys put his head out of the window.

'Mr Bloggs,' he shouted. 'Maybe there's a bird's nest in one of the drainpipes. That happened to us, once.'

Mr Bloggs was ready to try anything, so he went away to look in the drainpipes. Melanie Brown suddenly remembered her shorts! She ran to the door, but Miss Bradley called her.

'You can't go out in all this rain,' she said.

'But I've left something out there.'

'Well, it will have to stay there until the rain stops. Now find a comic to read.'

Melanie Brown found a comic, but she did not read it. She watched out of the window for Mr Bloggs. He went past, at last, carrying a very wet pair of green shorts. Melanie Brown remembered that her name was in the shorts. So they would soon know who had blocked up the drainpipe, and made the gutter overflow!

Later that afternoon, when the rain had stopped, the headmistress came in. She had Melanie Brown's shorts in her hand, and she spoke to Miss Bradley. Melanie Brown had to tell them how the shorts came to be in the drainpipe. They were both very annoyed. Then the headmistress took Melanie Brown along to see Mr Bloggs, and to tell him she was sorry.

'I didn't mean to cause you all that bother,' she told him.

'Well, see it doesn't happen again,' he said, and she promised.

Next time they went on the big apparatus, Melanie Brown was the first one to get changed.

'Do you know,' she said to Denise, 'I've changed my mind about green. I think it does suit me, after all!'

Melanie Brown and the Christmas Concert

As soon as Melanie Brown knew that there was going to be a Christmas concert she made up her mind she would be in it. Miss Bradley told them every class would be in the concert and all the mothers and fathers could come and watch. Melanie Brown was so excited she jumped up from her chair.

'Miss Bradley, I can sing. I'm good at singing. Can I be in the concert?'

'Sit down, Melanie,' said Miss Bradley, smiling. 'I haven't finished telling you about it yet.'

But Melanie Brown would *not* sit down.

'I can dance, Miss Bradley,' she said. 'Can I dance in the concert?'

'I've told you to sit down, Melanie. No one else is calling out. Please wait until I've finished.'

Melanie Brown sat down, but then jumped up again.

'I know, Miss Bradley. I can say a nursery rhyme. I can say Jack and Jill – '

'Melanie Brown!' said Miss Bradley, in a very cross voice. 'If you don't sit down and be quiet, you won't be in the concert at all!'

The children looked at Melanie Brown and she went

very red. She sat down as quickly as she could and tried to listen quietly while Miss Bradley told them about the concert.

She told them that the top class was going to sing some songs, the middle class was going to do some dances and their class was going to act a nativity play.

'A nativity play tells the story of the first Christmas and the birth of baby Jesus in the stable,' said Miss Bradley. 'We will act the story and sing some carols. Some of you will be dressed up as certain people in the story. Others will help with the singing.'

Then she began to choose the children for the different parts.

'Please, Miss Bradley, can I be Jesus?' asked Melanie Brown.

'No, dear. No one is going to be Jesus because Jesus is only a tiny baby in this play. Now be quiet, please.'

Denise was chosen to be Mary and Nicholas to be Joseph. Three boys would be the shepherds and another three the wise men. A few girls would be angels and the rest of the class would sing carols.

'Please, Miss Bradley, can I be the ox?' Melanie Brown asked hopefully. 'I can moo like an ox.'

'We aren't having any animals in it, dear. You are going to sing carols.'

'But Miss Bradley, I can't sing, but I *can* moo.'

'Stop being silly, Melanie. You told us just a moment ago that you were good at singing.'

Melanie Brown gave up. She sat in her chair with a very grumpy face while Miss Bradley told each of the children what to say, where to sit or stand, and when to move from one place to another. In spite of herself, she had to admit it sounded very exciting. In fact, it was the most interesting thing that had happened since she started school. She soon forgot her disappointment at not being an ox, and as the days went by she tried really hard, until she was the first to remember every word of the carols. Miss Bradley was very pleased with her.

But then something happened to make Melanie Brown naughty again. One day Miss Bradley brought a big cardboard box into the room and began to take out the clothes the children were going to wear.

Denise was to be Mary, so she wore a long blue

gown, with a white shawl over her head. Nicholas was to be Joseph and he wore a long green robe tied with a silk cord.

The shepherds were given ragged tunics and the angels long white gowns, but the wise men had velvet cloaks and crowns. It was the crowns that made Melanie Brown feel naughty again.

The crowns were made of cardboard covered with silver paper, decorated with jewels made from wine gums. Red wine gums were rubies and green wine gums were emeralds. The children gasped with delight when they saw the crowns, and Melanie Brown gasped louder than anyone else. She badly wanted to be a wise man so that she could wear one. She got up from her chair and went out to Miss Bradley.

'Miss Bradley, I don't want to be an ox any more,' she said firmly.

'No, dear, I know you don't.'

'I want to be a wise man.'

'Well, you can't be a wise man, Melanie, because you're a girl, and anyway you're a singer.'

'But I want to wear a crown.'

Miss Bradley reached into the box and pulled out some silver bands.

'Look,' she said, 'silver head-bands are for the singers. Try one on, Melanie. I'm sure it will look very nice on you.'

Melanie Brown took the silver head-band and walked over to the mirror. She banged it on her head and pulled a horrible face at herself in the mirror. The other singers put their head-bands on and they really

did look charming. Even Melanie Brown thought so, but she did not want to admit it. However, she kept the head-band on and went into the hall with the others to rehearse the play on the stage. It was fun.

Melanie Brown was longing for the day of the concert because her mother and father were coming and she wanted them to see her on the stage. Then they would see how grown-up she was now she was a schoolgirl.

The day of the concert came at last. Melanie Brown thought the morning would never pass and she was so excited she could hardly eat her dinner.

When it was time to start dressing up Melanie Brown's legs began to feel like jelly. She was glad she did not have any words to say, because she was so nervous she felt sure she would have forgotten them.

Miss Bradley was busy helping the children to get ready, but suddenly she glanced out of the window.

'Shh!' she said to the children. 'Look outside! The mothers and fathers are arriving. You must all be much quieter.'

Melanie Brown was standing next to Christopher, watching for their mothers and fathers to arrive. Christopher was a kind little boy and he said, 'Shall we change over for a little while? You can wear my crown and I'll wear your head-band.'

Of course, Melanie Brown was only too pleased, and before she knew what was happening she was in front of the mirror with the beautiful silver crown on her head. The longer she looked at herself the more certain she was that the crown looked better on her than it did on Christopher. If *only* she could have been a wise man! She suddenly felt angry with Miss Bradley, and jealous of Christopher, and she did a very naughty thing. She pulled off one of the red wine gums and put it in her mouth. It tasted rather odd, but she thought that must be the glue that Miss Bradley had used to stick it on. Then she ate one of the green wine gums, then another red one, and another green one, until they had all gone.

At that moment she heard Miss Bradley's voice.

'Christopher, where's your crown? Put it on quickly. It's nearly time to go into the hall.'

Melanie Brown snatched off the crown, and Christopher picked it up. He stared, and his eyes filled with tears.

Miss Bradley hurried over to them.

'Come along, get into line you two. Why, whatever is the matter, Christopher?'

When she saw the crown she was very angry, but there was no time to say anything just then. She was too busy trying to console Christopher. It would never do for one of the three wise men to be crying when he went to find Jesus.

'Cheer up, Christopher,' she said, drying his tears with a paper handkerchief. 'I think I've got some Smarties in the sweet tin. I'll stick some of those on the crown. They will look just as pretty.'

And sure enough, they did.

Then it was time for the nativity play, which was a great success. When it was all over the mothers and fathers clapped their hands for a long time, they had enjoyed it so much.

That evening, when Melanie Brown was eating her supper, her mother said, 'You sang beautifully in the concert, Melanie, but why weren't you wearing a silver head-band like the other singers?'

And, do you know, Melanie Brown had been so upset after spoiling Christopher's crown that she had forgotten to put her head-band on again. It made her sad, just to think about it.

But I think it was her own fault, don't you?

Melanie Brown and the Dentist

Melanie Brown always made a dreadful fuss when her mother took her to the dentist. I don't know why, but she did. The dentist was a friendly man, who smiled and joked with her, but still she did not like him. She did not even like the chair that tipped up and down. And she always made a fuss. She kicked and cried and screamed. The poor man could never persuade her to open her mouth, not even a tiny bit, so no one knew whether any of her teeth needed mending.

So when Miss Bradley told them one morning that the school dentist was coming to look at their teeth, Melanie Brown did not know what to do. She looked round to see if the other children would make a fuss.

Susan was clipping a sheet of paper on to the painting easel, Christopher was rolling up his sleeves by the sand-tray, and Denise was softening a large lump of plasticine. No one seemed to be worrying about the dentist.

She went over to the Wendy House, and looked in. Nicholas was there, pulling a white coat from the dressing-up box. He looked up.

'Do you want to play?' he asked.

'What are you playing – doctors?'

'No, dentists. I'm the dentist. You can be the mother if you like and the doll can be your little girl.'

'I don't want to play dentists,' said Melanie Brown crossly. 'It's a silly game.'

'All right, don't play,' said Nicholas. 'I'll ask Paula.'

Melanie Brown sat down on a chair, put her thumb in her mouth, and watched him crossly. Paula, it seemed, *wanted* to play 'dentists' and they both disappeared inside the Wendy House.

Melanie Brown began to swing her legs, kicking the leg of the desk.

She thought it was very mean of Paula to play with Nicholas. She jumped up and looked in at the window of the Wendy House.

'I'm going to play with the farm, Paula,' she told her. 'Do you want to play with me?'

'No, thank you,' said Paula politely. 'I want to play "dentists".'

Melanie Brown was so annoyed that she poked her tongue out at them and went back to her chair. No one took any notice of her so she began to kick the leg of the desk again, as hard as she could. Miss Bradley heard her and looked up.

'Don't make that noise, Melanie Brown,' she said sharply. 'Find something to do.'

So she wandered over to the sand-tray where Christopher was making tunnels in the sand.

'These tunnels are caves,' he said. 'I'm pretending the sea comes in and fills them with water. Do you want to play?'

'Tunnels are stupid,' said Melanie Brown, and she

reached into the sand-tray and pushed in the tunnels. She thought Christopher would start to cry but he did not. He hit her on the hand instead, with the rubber spade. Melanie Brown screamed and began to cry. She cried as loudly as she could because she did not want

Miss Bradley to hear Christopher when he told her about the tunnels. But Miss Bradley did manage to hear and she said, 'Stop crying, you naughty girl. It was your own fault. What is the matter with you this morning? You're not usually so silly.'

And she gave her a book and a pencil and some tracing-paper. But Melanie Brown did not want to trace a picture, so she poked the pencil through the paper and made a hole in it. Then she scribbled on the back of the chair and dropped the pencil down the back of the cupboard. She was determined to be a real nuisance.

Just then, however, the classroom door opened and a lady came in. She was the prettiest lady Melanie Brown had ever seen. She had brown eyes and black hair which curled softly all over her head, and she wore a necklace of pink and white beads. Her dress was pink and her shoes were white with tiny white bows. Melanie Brown decided that as soon as she was grown-up she would look like that.

The lady talked to Miss Bradley and they both laughed a lot.

Then the lady looked at her watch and said, 'Well, give me ten minutes and then send the first six in,' and went out again.

Melanie Brown took a sheet of paper from the table and found her crayons. She began to draw a princess with short black curls and a pink dress and white shoes.

She was still busy drawing when Miss Bradley called her out to the front, with Stephen and Susan and three other children. They went through the hall and into the room where the teachers had their coffee. There, to Melanie Brown's surprise, was the pretty lady, wearing a white coat and holding a bundle of cards. Miss Bradley told the lady the children's names and each child was given her own card. The pretty lady was the dentist!

Melanie Brown was first. She sat on a chair and opened her mouth and the lady looked at all her teeth with a little mirror on a stick.

'What nice teeth,' said the lady, smiling. 'Do you clean them every morning and every night?'

Melanie Brown nodded shyly.

'Good girl. Next one, please,' said the dentist, and that was all. It was almost disappointing. Melanie Brown began to wonder why she had always made such a fuss.

When she got back to the classroom she finished her picture of the princess and put it in her coat pocket to show her mother. Then she ran over to the Wendy House and asked Nicholas if she could play 'dentists'.

Melanie Brown and the Sugar Mice

One morning the children went into the hall, and saw a big, big Christmas tree. It was the biggest Christmas tree that Melanie Brown had ever seen. It stood in one corner and it was so wide it touched the walls with its branches. It was so high that it nearly touched the ceiling. The roots were planted in a big red pot, and beside the tub was a box full of decorations. Melanie Brown was so excited that she forgot the words of the hymn. She turned round so many times to look at it that the headmistress told her to pay attention.

Later that morning Miss Bradley told them that they were going to have a Christmas Party.

'We will have games and a party tea,' she said, 'and then one of Father Christmas's fairies will give every child a present. There will be a small present on the tree, too, for you to take home to your brothers and sisters.'

All the children clapped with delight – all except Melanie Brown, that is. She felt cheated because she did not have any brothers or sisters. Jennifer had a baby brother, and Christopher had two sisters. The more she thought about it, the more she decided it was not fair. So she made herself look as miserable as possible, and waited for Miss Bradley to notice her.

'What's the matter, Melanie?' said Miss Bradley at last. 'Don't you like parties?'

Melanie Brown tried to squeeze out a few tears but they would not come.

'It's not fair,' she said. 'I haven't got any sisters or brothers, so I won't have a present off the tree.'

'But you will have a big present from the fairy,' said Miss Bradley patiently, 'and the presents on the tree will only be small presents.'

Jennifer asked her what the small presents would be.

'Sugar mice, I think,' she said. 'Now, that's enough about the party. We must do some work.'

That night, as she lay in bed, Melanie Brown thought about the sugar mice, and the more she thought about them the more determined she became to get one, somehow. So the next day, when it was news-time, Melanie Brown stood up. 'My Mummy is having a baby,' she said.

'Is she?' said Miss Bradley, surprised. 'It will be nice for you to have someone to play with, won't it? When is the baby coming?'

'The day of the party,' said Melanie Brown, 'so may I have a sugar mouse?'

'Melanie Brown!' laughed Miss Bradley. 'You are making all that up, just so that you can have a sugar mouse. What a greedy girl!'

So that was no good. But the next morning, as luck would have it, Melanie Brown found herself right next to the Christmas tree at prayer-time. When everyone closed their eyes for the prayer, she kept hers open. Slowly she reached up and her fingers closed round a little pink mouse. With a quick tug she tried to pull it down, but – oh dear! The mouse was tied on too

tightly. The branch shook, and all the silver balls danced about. The headmistress heard them rustling and opened her eyes, to see what was going on. Quick as a flash Melanie Brown closed her eyes again. So that was no good, either.

But Melanie Brown was a very determined little girl, and she had made up her mind to have a mouse. After prayers, Miss Bradley marked the register, and asked her to take it to the headmistress. On the way back Melanie Brown looked into the hall. There was no one there. She ran straight to the tree, stood on tiptoe, and bit the head off a yellow mouse. It was

delicious! She bit the head off a white mouse, and that was delicious, too. So was the pink mouse's head. They were so good that before she knew what she was doing, she had bitten off *all* the heads.

Then she ate a whole mouse and that was a bad mistake, because she forgot about the string tail. As she swallowed it, it stuck in her throat. She thought she was going to choke. She was coughing and spluttering when Mrs Jones came into the hall, and saw the poor little headless mice. She was very angry. She gave Melanie Brown a pat on the back, to make her cough up the string, and then took her to the headmistress.

'Melanie Brown, I'm surprised at you,' said the headmistress. 'You are a naughty, greedy girl. You do not deserve to go to the party, so you will go home instead.'

And that is what happened. Melanie Brown never did like sugar mice, after that.

Melanie Brown and the Policemen

Melanie Brown woke up one morning. She felt sure something exciting was going to happen, but she could not remember what it was. She washed, dressed and ate her breakfast so quickly that she had a few moments to spare, and her mother said she could play in the garden with her ball. Because she was so excited, she bounced her ball very hard and it bounced right over the gate and into the road. Melanie Brown rushed after it. She didn't stop to see if there was any traffic coming, but ran straight into the road. HONK! HONK! HONK! Car brakes squealed as a large black car pulled up close beside her. A man leaned out of the window and shouted angrily at her.

'Lucky for you I've got good brakes, or you might have been run over. Don't you know you should never run into the road?'

Melanie Brown hung her head and didn't answer.

'Just you remember in future, young lady,' said the driver, and he drove away down the road.

Poor Melanie Brown was very upset. She picked up the ball and took it back indoors.

She was still very quiet when she arrived at school, and Miss Bradley wondered what was the matter, and

asked her if she felt ill. Melanie Brown shook her head.

'Well, cheer up then, dear. The policemen are coming today to give us a demonstration on road safety. Have you forgotten?'

So *that* was the exciting thing she had been trying to remember!

When it was time for the demonstration they all went into the big hall, and sat in rows, leaving a big space down the middle. There were three policemen in dark blue uniforms, with shiny silver buttons, and black shiny shoes. They did look tall. Melanie Brown felt very small and she sat very still.

Then one of the policemen talked to them about crossing the road, and he told them to pretend that the space in the middle of the hall was the road. He told two girls to walk up and down and pretend that they were going for a walk.

'They are quite safe,' he said, 'because the road is empty. There is no traffic at the moment. But look – whatever is this coming in?'

He pointed to the hall door and to everyone's amazement they saw a *car* coming in. A real car was coming in through the hall door! It was not a big car, of course, with an engine to drive it along, but it was quite big and it had pedals. It was bright red, with shiny silver bumpers and a black steering wheel. It had two headlamps and the seats were made of red leather. The policeman said he was going to choose someone to drive it! Someone who was sitting up nice and straight! Melanie Brown sat up *very* straight, but so did everyone else, and the policeman chose a boy called Simon. They all watched him climb into the car and thought him the luckiest boy in the school.

Then the two girls pretended to walk in the road again. Simon pedalled very hard and the car went along and bumped into one of the girls. She fell over and pretended she was hurt.

'Oh dear,' said the policeman. 'There's been an accident. I wonder why that happened. Does anyone know?'

Melanie Brown's hand went up straight away, so the policeman asked her to tell him.

'They were walking in the road,' said Melanie Brown, 'and not looking where they were going.'

'Good girl,' said the policeman.

Next, the policeman unrolled a big carpet. At least, it looked like a carpet when it was rolled up, but when it was unrolled it was striped in black and white. It was a pretend zebra-crossing. They laid it on the floor across the road, and the policeman brought in another car! This one was blue and silver with brown leather seats.

'Now, come along, little girl,' said the policeman to Melanie Brown. 'You were quick with your answer just now, so you can drive the blue car for us.'

Melanie Brown stood up and walked over to the car in a sort of dream. She sat on the brown leather seat and her feet just reached to the pedals in the bottom of the car.

Then they pretended that three children wanted to cross the road and the two cars had to drive along and stop to let them walk over the zebra-crossing. It was great fun pedalling along, just like a lady in a real car.

Denise was chosen next, to be a 'school-crossing lady'.

She dressed up in a white coat and carried a pole with a notice on the top which said 'STOP – CHILDREN CROSSING'. When the drivers saw the notice they had to stop while the children crossed the road.

Lastly they wheeled in a small ice-cream van and chose Christopher to be the driver. The policeman told them never to run across the road to an ice-cream van. Then he said, 'Keep looking both ways, and if it's safe walk across the road.'

The children promised to remember, and at last it

was over. The children were sorry to say 'good-bye' to the friendly policemen.

That afternoon, Miss Bradley told them there would be a prize for the best painting about road safety.

Melanie Brown painted a very big blue car and a

little girl waiting to cross the road. There was a very fat school-crossing lady in the picture, too, and squashed up very small in one corner there was an ice-cream van.

The headmistress thought it was the best and she gave Melanie Brown the prize. It was a small shiny blue torch, the same colour as the car!

PART TWO

for

JONATHAN

and the children of

RIDGEWELL SCHOOL

Melanie Brown Climbs a Tree

Melanie Brown was nearly six years old and she went to the village school. She had a nice teacher whose name was Miss Bradley and they understood each other very well. She also had a great many friends but her favourite friend was a boy called Christopher. He was Melanie Brown's boy-friend, and they always walked home together after school.

One day Christopher had a bad cold and had to stay away from school, so when it was home time there was no one for Melanie Brown to walk with. She hated walking on her own, so she looked around for someone else to walk with. But no one was as nice as Christopher and she spent such a long time trying to make up her mind that suddenly there were only two boys left. They were Nigel and Dennis, two of the boys in the top class.

'I'll walk home with you,' she told them.

They looked at her in dismay.

'We don't walk home with girls!' said Nigel. 'They're soppy!'

'Girls are *not* soppy,' said Melanie Brown indignantly. 'And I'll have to walk with you because all the others have gone, and I don't like walking by myself.'

'Well, you can't walk with us,' said Nigel, 'because

61

we're not going home.'

'Not going home?' said Melanie Brown. 'Why aren't you going home?'

'Because we're going to do something else first, and it's a secret, so go away!'

But, of course, that made her all the more determined to stay. They shouted at her, and they pushed her away, but she took no notice.

'Tell me the secret, then,' she said, 'and I'll go away.'

They glared at her angrily, and then whispered together. At last Dennis said, 'We're going to climb a tree.'

Melanie Brown's eyes opened wide. She had never climbed a tree!

'I'll come with you,' she said, and nothing they could say or do could make her change her mind.

Behind the school kitchen was a big old oak tree. It was perfect for climbing because it had wide, spreading branches. Melanie Brown looked up into its green leaves and was quite delighted. She imagined how it would be to sit up there, hidden from view.

Dennis went up first. He went up quickly and easily, until suddenly his foot slipped. Melanie Brown gave a little scream.

'Shh!' warned Nigel. 'We're not supposed to be round here, so be quiet.'

She looked round anxiously.

'But there's no one to hear us,' she said.

'The teachers haven't gone home yet,' said Nigel.

Soon both the boys were up in the tree, looking down at Melanie Brown.

'If you don't help me up,' she said, 'I'll scream and scream and scream until someone hears me, and then I'll tell them you're up the tree!'

The boys muttered some very nasty things about girls but Dennis climbed down and helped her up. In no time at all she was sitting astride a wide branch, her head among the leaves. It was wonderful!

'It's just like a tree house,' she said breathlessly. 'Oh, let's play mothers and fathers!'

The boys looked at her without enthusiasm.

'This is our house,' she said, 'and I'm the mother, and you're the father and the uncle, and you have to go to work, while I make the dinner. These leaves can be the dinner – '

'We are *not* playing mothers and fathers,' said Nigel grimly, 'so shut up.'

Melanie Brown ignored him.

'That big branch can be the bedroom, and this is the kitchen and this is an upstairs flat because it's so high . . .'

Dennis and Nigel exchanged despairing looks, then quietly they began to climb down from the tree. She watched them go.

'That's right,' she said happily. 'You go to work, and when you come back the dinner will be ready.'

But the boys had had enough of Melanie Brown for one day. They climbed down from the tree, and they wandered off along the lane, and they did *not* come back. They left Melanie Brown in the tree all on her own!

Melanie Brown waited and waited for the father and the uncle to come home from work, but, of course, they never did. At first she was annoyed with them, then she began to get worried, and finally she got very frightened and tried to climb down but the tree was too high and she was too small. She began to wonder if she would be there all night, with the bats and the owls!

'Help me, someone,' she shouted. 'I'm up in the tree! Help me!'

There was no answer, so she shouted again and again, until at last she heard footsteps, and there was Mr Bloggs the caretaker, looking up at her in amazement.

'Blow me down!' he said. 'If it's not Melanie Brown!

I might have known it! Never met a girl like you for getting into mischief. I suppose I'll have to go and get my ladder.' And he went off to fetch it, grumbling to himself about 'young people today' not being what they were in his day.

When he came back Melanie Brown's mother was with him. She had come up to the school to look for Melanie Brown, when she did not come home from school. Mr Bloggs rested the ladder against the tree,

but still Melanie Brown was afraid to climb down. Mr Bloggs snorted. 'I suppose I'll have to carry you down,' he said. 'I'll give you a fireman's lift, that's what I'll do. Didn't know I used to be a fireman, did you?'

She agreed that she did not know. He went up the ladder and carried her safely down.

'I've got a photograph at home, of me in my fireman's uniform. I'll show it to you some time,' he said.

She said that she would like to see it. Then Mrs Brown thanked him for all his help, and they said 'goodbye' and hurried away down the lane. When they told Mr Brown what had happened he bought some tobacco for Mr Bloggs to smoke in his pipe. Melanie Brown gave it to him when she passed his cottage next morning, on her way to school. Mr Bloggs showed her the photograph, and she thought he looked very handsome in his uniform.

They have been good friends ever since.

Melanie Brown
and the Harvest Festival

Melanie Brown went home from school feeling very important. She had a note in her pocket which Miss Bradley had given her. She had kept it safely in her pocket all day without losing it. It was about the Harvest Festival. The headmistress had told them all about it.

'Autumn is harvest time,' she said. 'We want to thank God for all the good things he sends us. Fruit and vegetables and flowers. We say "thank you" by taking some of the things to church. Then, after the service, we give the things to old people who do not have much money.'

Melanie Brown thought it was a wonderful idea, and so did her mother.

'We'll ask Daddy if he can find you the two biggest apples on the tree,' she said, and of course, Daddy said he would. He took a ladder and climbed up into the branches of the apple tree. Melanie Brown held out her skirt, and he dropped the two biggest apples into it – one at a time, of course, so they did not bruise. She washed the apples under the tap and polished them with a soft cloth. They were big and green and shiny and she could hardly wait to show them to the other children.

She set off along the lane next morning carrying the apples very carefully. Soon Christopher joined her. He had a large cabbage tucked under his arm. His big blue eyes opened wide when he saw the big green apples.

'What giant apples!' he said.

She told him they were from her own tree.

'I wish I had an apple tree,' said Christopher wistfully. 'I love apples.'

Feeling suddenly generous Melanie Brown handed him one of the big green apples.

'You can have this one,' she said. 'I'm sure the old people won't mind.'

Christopher smiled one of his biggest smiles and took a large bite. Then he pulled an awful face.

'Sour!' he said briefly.

Melanie Brown took it back and handed him the other one to try. That was sour, too.

'They must be cooking apples,' he said. They

looked at the two big apples, each with a large bite out of it. Without a word Christopher tossed his over the hedge into the pond – splash. Melanie Brown's apple followed it with another splash!

'Now I haven't got anything for Harvest Festival,' said Melanie Brown, 'and it's all your fault!'

Before they could start to argue Denise ran up to them. She had a bundle of onions in a polythene bag. 'Aren't you bringing anything?' she asked Melanie Brown.

'Of course!' said Melanie Brown. 'I'm bringing mine tomorrow – so it will be nice and fresh.'

That evening she told her mother what had happened to the apples.

'You are a silly girl,' said her mother. 'Never mind. I'll find you something else for tomorrow, but it won't be apples because it's raining and I'm not going down the garden to get all wet.'

Next morning she gave Melanie Brown a small basket. Inside were a packet of biscuits, a jelly, and a big brown egg.

'That is all I can spare,' she said, 'so take care of it.'

Melanie Brown promised she would and set off for school once more. Half-way along the lane she realized that no one had joined her.

'I must be early,' she said to herself and decided to stop and have a closer look at the biscuits. There was a chocolate one and a wafer and one with icing on it and the more Melanie Brown looked at them the more she felt sure that the old people would not like them because they were too sweet. Melanie Brown's grand-mother didn't like sweet biscuits and *she* was old!

'I'll just eat the sweet ones,' she told herself, 'and I'll leave the plain ones.'

It didn't seem quite right to stand in the lane eating the Harvest Festival biscuits, so she climbed over the gate into the field and sat down by the pond with her back against a tree. Now no one passing in the lane could see her. She opened the packet of biscuits and began to eat them. It was very pleasant by the pond with the sunlight glinting on the water. She could hear

voices in the lane and smiled to think how surprised the children would be if they could see her. When she had eaten all the biscuits she opened the jelly. It was in little squares, so she tasted a square and decided to eat that, too!

As she popped the last square into her mouth she suddenly noticed how quiet it was. There were no more voices in the lane. She jumped to her feet and the basket tumbled out of her lap. The big, brown egg rolled out and fell into the water, out of sight among the weeds.

'Well,' said Melanie Brown, 'that's that!'

She tossed the basket into a clump of stinging nettles and ran back to the gate. She ran along the lane to school and found the playground empty. The classroom was empty, too. She ran back into the lane and on to the church but before she reached the door the sound of music filled the air and she recognized the tune of 'All things bright and beautiful' which was her favourite hymn.

'They've started without me!' she told herself indignantly and hurried up to the door. She did mean to go in, but at the last moment her courage failed her. They might ask her about the biscuits and the jelly and the egg! Slowly she turned and made her way to a wooden seat by the path. She decided to wait for them instead and sat on the edge of the seat, swinging her legs.

'I wonder – ' she thought happily, 'I wonder what I'll bring for Harvest Festival next year!'

Melanie Brown's
First School Photograph

As soon as she heard the word 'photographer' Melanie Brown pricked up her ears. She didn't always pay a great deal of attention when Miss Bradley was talking to them, but this time she thought it sounded interesting.

'He won't be here until after dinner,' Miss Bradley told them, 'so try to keep yourselves clean and tidy.'

'Are we all going to be in the same photograph?' asked Paula.

'No,' said Miss Bradley. 'He will take a photograph of every child separately, except where there are brothers and sisters in the school. Then he will take a group.'

'But my sister's in the top class,' said Nicholas anxiously.

'It won't make any difference,' said Miss Bradley. 'We shall get all the children in each family together.'

Susan pulled a face.

'I don't want to be in a photograph with my brother,' she said. 'He's awful! I want to be on my own.'

'Well, you can't,' said Miss Bradley patiently. 'It would be too expensive for your mother and father to have to buy two photographs.'

'They're rich!' said Susan, but Miss Bradley only laughed and told them to remember what she had said about keeping clean.

Melanie Brown went straight into the cloakroom and looked at herself in the mirror. Her thick brown hair was tied in two bunches. She looked thoughtfully at the ribbons.

'Please may I go home?' she asked Miss Bradley. 'I want to get my best pink ribbons – they're pink velvet!'

'But, Melanie,' said Miss Bradley, 'whatever is wrong with those red ones you are wearing? They look very smart. Anyway, there is no time for you to go home. The dinner is almost ready. Hurry up and wash your hands.'

Melanie Brown picked up the soap and put it down again. She crossed to the mirror and looked at herself once more.

'I could take off the ribbons and wear my hair loose!' she said. 'Or I could have a pony tail – or two little plaits?'

Miss Bradley laughed.

'Melanie,' she said, 'you look very nice as you are. Your mother will want a photograph of you as you are at school. You can dress up and wear you hair differently when you have a photograph taken at home. Now do get a move on with that washing. We're all waiting for you.'

Melanie Brown was very displeased. She sat through dinner with a very grumpy face and wouldn't smile, not even when she saw that it was ginger pudding which was her favourite. Then, suddenly, she had another idea. As soon as the last plate was neatly stacked on the trolley she ran to find Christopher and tell him her idea. She found him sitting on the fence, so she climbed up beside him.

'Would you like to be in my photograph?' she asked him sweetly.

'Can't!' he said briefly.

'I'll ask Miss Bradley,' she urged, 'if you want to be in it.'

'But I'm not your brother,' said Christopher, 'and you're not my sister, so we aren't the same family – so we can't.'

'You are my best boy-friend,' said Melanie Brown, but Christopher said that Miss Bradley hadn't mentioned boy-friends.

'She forgot!' said Melanie Brown airily. 'I'll go and remind her.'

She found Miss Bradley cleaning the blackboard, and explained her idea.

'I'm sorry,' said Miss Bradley. 'A best boy-friend is not the same as family. Your mother wouldn't want a photograph with Christopher in it – and Christopher's mother won't want one with you in it! Do stop fussing and go out to play like a good girl.'

But Melanie Brown was *not* a good girl. She did not go out to play. She flew into a tantrum instead! She sobbed and wailed and argued and pleaded. She tossed her head and stamped her feet – she even shouted at Miss Bradley. But Miss Bradley just went on cleaning the blackboard and didn't take any notice at all. At

last Melanie Brown had to stop because she was worn out and tired of all the noise she was making, so she went into the Wendy House to recover.

Of course, when the photographer came she had her photograph taken without any fuss and she waited eagerly for the results. They came the next week in a big envelope. The photographs were in colour and each one was in a little white cardboard frame. The children were delighted – all except Melanie Brown.

The little girl in *her* cardboard frame looked very disagreeable and had red eyes from all that crying! Hastily she tucked the photograph into her satchel so that no one else should see how awful she looked. She had a nasty feeling that her mother and father were not going to be very pleased with her very first school photograph!

Melanie Brown and the Best Doll

Melanie Brown had a best doll. She had three dolls altogether – an old rag doll called Susie; a fairy doll who had lost her wand; and a baby doll called Sarah. Sarah was her best doll, because she had real golden hair, long eyelashes, and blue eyes that opened and shut. Grandmother knitted lots of pretty clothes for Sarah, and Melanie Brown was very proud of her.

One day she put Sarah's best dress on, and took her to school. When she went into the playground all the other girls crowded round to see the best doll.

'Isn't she lovely,' said Jennifer. 'May I hold her, please?'

'You can if you don't drop her,' said Melanie Brown, and she watched anxiously while Jennifer held Sarah. Then, of course, all the girls wanted to hold her, but the whistle blew and it was time to go into school.

Melanie Brown showed Sarah to Miss Bradley.

'Oh Melanie, what a lovely doll,' said Miss Bradley, 'and what a pretty dress she's wearing.'

'My Granny knitted it,' said Melanie Brown proudly.

'Your Granny must be very good at knitting.'

'She is.'

'Well, leave the doll here until we come out of prayers and then you can play with her.'

As soon as they were back in the classroom Melanie Brown took Sarah into the Wendy House and Denise, Paula and Christopher went in too. They played 'mothers and fathers' and it was great fun.

When it was time to do some writing Melanie Brown saw that the chair next to hers was empty because Pat was away from school. She asked Miss Bradley if Sarah could sit there and Miss Bradley said, 'Yes,' so the best doll sat next to her.

'I do hope Sarah won't talk too much,' said Miss Bradley, and that made all the children laugh.

At story-time Sarah sat on Melanie Brown's lap. It really was a very happy morning. At dinner-time, however, Denise went home and brought back *her* best doll. It was a 'walkie-talkie' doll called Catherine Elizabeth and all the girls began to admire Catherine Elizabeth instead of Sarah. Melanie Brown was not at all pleased.

'Catherine Elizabeth is very clever,' Denise told them. 'When I pull this cord she talks. Listen.'

She pulled a cord and the doll began to talk.

'What a silly, squeaky voice!' said Melanie Brown, but no one was listening to her. Then they all watched the doll walk.

'What a funny way to walk!' said Melanie Brown. 'She can't even bend her legs!'

Denise glared at her.

'Well, your doll can't even walk *or* talk, so there!'

Melanie Brown was so upset she took Sarah away

to the other side of the playground, and sat down on the grass. She felt very miserable.

When they went back into school Miss Bradley saw the other doll.

'Another lovely doll!' she said. 'You two girls will be able to play together at play-time.'

But Melanie Brown and Denise just glared at each other and said nothing.

Later that afternoon, when they were in the hall, Miss Bradley asked Melanie Brown to run back to the classroom and fetch her music book. Melanie Brown loved to be chosen to run errands and she hurried to find the right book so that she could show the children how clever she was, but the first thing she saw when she entered the classroom was the 'walkie-talkie' doll, sitting on Denise's chair. It really was a very pretty doll. Melanie Brown forgot all about the music book and picked up Catherine Elizabeth. She pulled the cord and listened. 'Mama, I'm a good girl – Tell me a story – I like sweeties – I don't want to go to bed – '

Then she walked the doll round the classroom until

79

she came to her own best doll. Poor Sarah didn't seem exciting any more. Melanie Brown shook the 'walkie-talkie' doll hard.

'It's all your fault, you horrid thing!' she said angrily and she shook it harder. Suddenly there was a funny noise inside the doll's head and Melanie Brown saw that the eyes had gone crooked! Carefully she poked her finger into the eyes to try to straighten them but instead they fell right in! It was terrible. Melanie Brown stared at the doll. She looked ugly without any eyes. Not nearly as pretty as Sarah. Melanie Brown didn't know whether to be glad or sorry. Quickly she sat the doll back on Denise's chair, found the music book, and went into the hall. She wondered what Denise would say when she saw Catherine Elizabeth but it was Jennifer who saw it first.

'Oh, Denise!' she cried. 'Look at your doll! She hasn't got any eyes – she looks horrible!'

Denise took one look and started to cry. Miss Bradley looked round at all the children. They were all staring at the doll except Melanie Brown who was staring at the floor with a very red face.

'How did it happen?' Miss Bradley asked, but Melanie Brown hung her head and wouldn't answer.

'Was it an accident?' she said, but still Melanie Brown said nothing. Miss Bradley sighed.

'You must tell Denise you are sorry,' she said, but Melanie Brown shook her head stubbornly and began to kick the table leg.

'Very well,' said Miss Bradley, 'you must stand out in front of the class in disgrace!'

Melanie Brown was still out in front of the class when it was time to go home, and she began to worry in case she was left there all night!

'I want to go home,' she said in a shaky voice.

'Not until you tell Denise you are sorry,' said Miss Bradley.

Melanie Brown marched up to Denise, who was changing her shoes in the cloakroom.

'SORRY!' she shouted, so loudly that poor Denise nearly jumped out of her skin!

'Not like that!' said Miss Bradley sternly. 'You must say it properly.'

Melanie Brown closed her eyes so that she wouldn't have to see Denise's face.

'I'm sorry,' she said, and although she didn't sound very sorry Miss Bradley thought it would have to do.

By the time Melanie Brown had changed her shoes and put on her coat and hat everyone else had gone home, so she had to walk down the lane on her own.

'Catherine Elizabeth!' she said to herself. 'What a silly name for a doll! Sarah is much nicer. Still, tomorrow I think I'll bring a book.'

Melanie Brown and the Eye-test

Melanie Brown's mother had two pairs of sun-glasses – one pair with blue frames, and one pair with black frames. Melanie Brown had none at all, and she thought it most unfair.

'Why can't *I* have a pair of sun-glasses?' she demanded crossly.

'You don't need any,' said Mrs Brown. 'I get a headache if the sun is very bright, so I wear them to protect my eyes from the glare.'

'I get headaches too,' said Melanie Brown. 'I get one whenever the sun shines. I've got one now.'

'But it's raining now,' said Mrs Brown, hiding a smile behind her hand.

Melanie Brown looked out of the window at the rain. 'Perhaps I need rain-glasses,' she said hopefully, but her mother only laughed. It was very discouraging.

Next morning, however, she had a pleasant surprise. The head-mistress told them that the school nurse was coming to test their eyes.

'My eyes are very good,' said Nicholas, when they were back in the classroom, 'because I eat a lot of carrots. I can see much further than my Dad.'

'I can see for a hundred miles!' said Christopher.

'I can see for two hundred miles!' said Denise, but no one quite believed her. Melanie Brown was just going to say that she could see for three hundred miles with one eye shut, when she had a much better idea. If she could not have any sun-glasses, then perhaps she could have a pair of real glasses.

'I can only see a little bit,' she told them sadly, 'and I get headaches every time it rains.'

They looked at her with interest.

'Every time it rains?' said Nicholas. 'Are you sure?'

'Of course I'm sure,' she said, 'and every time it's sunny.'

They considered this information for a moment.

'What about when it snows?' asked Christopher, at last.

Melanie Brown nodded proudly. 'And when it's foggy, or thundery,' she added.

Denise pointed her finger at Melanie Brown. 'You need glasses,' she said solemnly, and they all agreed. It was most exciting.

'Tell the nurse,' advised Denise, and Melanie Brown promised that she would. She could hardly wait for her turn to have her eyes tested. Nicholas went in first, and was soon back, looking very important.

'It's easy,' he told them. 'You have a piece of cardboard over one of your eyes, and you have to look at letters and pictures and say what they are. I got them all right,' he added proudly.

'I bet Melanie will get them all wrong,' said Christopher gloomily, and they all agreed.

At last her name was called and she went into the hall, followed by the sympathetic glances of her friends. The school nurse smiled at her.

'Hullo, Melanie,' she said. 'I'll just ask you a few questions first. Do you ever get headaches?'

Melanie Brown told her that she did, and she told her about when it rained and snowed, and was thundery or foggy. The nurse listened politely, and then handed her a small piece of cardboard.

'Just hold this over your right eye, dear, and tell me which letter I'm holding up.'

She moved away across the room, and held up the letter 'M'. Melanie Brown screwed up her eyes, and pretended she couldn't see.

' "B" ,' she said.

The nurse held up the letter 'F'.

' "O" ,' said Melanie Brown.

The nurse gave her a long look.

'Don't you know your letters, dear?' she asked, but without waiting for an answer she held up a picture

of an elephant.

'Now dear, can you tell me what this is?'

'A pig,' said Melanie Brown although she knew it was not a pig.

The nurse held up a fish.

'A chicken,' said Melanie Brown, who was beginning to enjoy herself.

'And this one?' said the nurse. It was a shoe.

'A tea-pot,' said Melanie Brown, 'and please may I have my glasses now?'

But the nurse said she didn't have any with her.

'You go back to the classroom,' she said, 'and I'll come and have a word with your teacher.'

Melanie Brown went back to the classroom feeling

very cross. Her friends gathered round her excitedly.

'Where are your glasses?' asked Nicholas, and she had to explain that the nurse didn't have any with her.

'Poor old Melanie!' said Denise. 'Have you still got a headache?'

Melanie Brown nodded. 'It's getting worse!' she said. They all began to comfort her and Christopher gave her a jelly baby to eat at play-time. She began to enjoy herself. Then the nurse came into the room and spoke to Miss Bradley and Miss Bradley called Melanie Brown out to the front. All the children listened eagerly.

'Nurse tells me you couldn't see any of the pictures,' said Miss Bradley. 'Is that so?'

Melanie Brown nodded.

'But you always seem to see the blackboard without any trouble,' said Miss Bradley. 'I can't understand it. Are you sure you couldn't see them?'

Melanie Brown nodded again.

'What a shame!' said Miss Bradley. 'Then we shall have to leave you behind when we go to the zoo on Friday because you won't be able to see the animals properly.'

'But I'll have my new glasses!' cried Melanie Brown.

The nurse shook her head.

'I'm afraid they won't be ready by Friday,' she said. 'It takes a long time to make a pair of glasses. Never mind, you will be able to go next year, I expect.'

Melanie Brown stared at her.

'Poor old Melanie!' said Christopher. 'She can't go to the zoo!'

Melanie Brown looked at him and then she looked at Miss Bradley – and then she looked at the nurse.

'It was a joke!' she said firmly. 'I was playing a joke!'

There was a long silence. Everyone waited to see what would happen next.

'A joke!' said Miss Bradley at last. 'Do you call it a joke to waste the nurse's time like that? I certainly don't. I call it naughtiness! You are a very bad girl! You don't deserve to go to the zoo!'

Melanie Brown frowned at her shoes and said nothing. Miss Bradley took her hand.

'You will have to have your eyes tested again,' she said, 'and I will come with you to make sure there's no more nonsense.'

Of course, Melanie Brown managed all the cards that time, so she didn't get a pair of glasses after all. And because she didn't want to miss the visit to the zoo, she tried extra hard to be good for the rest of the day. It was such an effort that by home-time she really did have a headache! Poor Melanie Brown!

Melanie Brown
and Woolly Brown Bear

The children were going to the zoo on Friday, so Miss Bradley talked to them about it on Thursday.

'You will need a packed lunch,' she said, 'a little pocket-money to spend, and a raincoat in case it is wet.'

'Can I bring my doll?' Denise asked, but Miss Bradley shook her head.

'No extras,' she said. 'If you have too many things to think about you are sure to lose something.'

All the children promised to remember but the next morning Melanie Brown marched into school with a teddy bear tucked under her arm.

'Ooh, look!' said Denise indignantly. 'Melanie Brown has brought an extra! It's not fair!'

'He's only small,' said Melanie Brown, smiling her sweetest smile. 'I call him Woolly Brown Bear because that's his name, but sometimes I call him Woolly Brown for short.'

'Well, *I* call him an extra,' said Miss Bradley, 'and you are not going to take him with you to the zoo.'

'Oh, please!' begged Melanie Brown. 'Woolly Brown Bear won't be any trouble, and I won't lose him – I promise! Please let me bring him!'

'No, Melanie,' said Miss Bradley firmly. 'There is

no reason why you should be allowed to bring a toy when none of the other children have brought their toys.'

And she turned away and started to mark the register to make sure that everyone was present who ought to be present.

Now Melanie Brown could be very determined at times. She had made up her mind to take Woolly Brown Bear and she was quite sure she wouldn't enjoy the zoo a bit without him. So when no one was looking she opened her satchel and stuffed him in on top of her sandwiches. When her name was called out she answered brightly and Miss Bradley was pleasantly surprised to see that she was not sulking. But of course she didn't know about Woolly Brown Bear!

'Right!' said Miss Bradley at last. 'Now it's time to go!'

The coach ride was great fun. Melanie Brown sat on the back seat with all her friends. There was so much to see and talk about she almost wished it could last for ever, but in no time at all they were at the zoo, and Miss Bradley was telling them not to wander too far in case they got lost.

The children had never seen so many animals. They saw tiny grey monkeys and large grey elephants; dainty gazelles and clumsy hippos; noisy parrots and silent snakes. They heard the lions roar and they laughed at the penguins and they watched the sealions being fed. Before they knew it the morning had slipped away and it was time to rest and eat their lunch. Thankfully they sat down under a big shady

tree and opened up their satchels. Melanie Brown had forgotten all about Woolly Brown Bear but the moment she opened her satchel he fell out on to the grass in front of everyone. Miss Bradley could hardly believe her eyes.

'Melanie Brown!' she cried. 'You really are the limit! Fancy bringing that bear with you after all I've said!'

But she didn't want to spoil the day with a grumble, so she said no more, but Melanie Brown knew what she was thinking and she went very red. Quickly she pushed Woolly Brown Bear down among the big roots of the tree and hoped Miss Bradley would forget about him. Then she turned her attention to her lunch, which was delicious. There were sausage rolls and egg sandwiches, an apple and a banana. There was a fizzy drink, too, which Miss Bradley opened for her with a special tin opener. By the time she had finished she was very full and felt rather sleepy, but Miss Bradley said they would have to look lively if they wanted to see everything before they went home.

The giraffes were much taller than Melanie Brown had imagined, and the buffaloes were much hairier. The camels were humpier, the chimpanzees were funnier, the . . . zebras . . . were . . . stripier . . . Melanie Brown was so tired her legs would hardly carry her along. Even Miss Bradley was weary.

'We'll just see the bears,' she said, 'and then we'll go back to the coach, and – what's the matter, Christopher?'

'It's Melanie – she's crying,' said Christopher. Melanie Brown lifted a tear-stained face.

'I've lost W-Woolly Brown B-Bear,' she sobbed. For once in her life Miss Bradley was speechless – but Denise wasn't!

'Serves you right!' she said. 'You shouldn't have brought him!'

'Denise is right,' sighed Miss Bradley, 'but that doesn't alter the fact that he's lost. Can you remember where you had him last?'

'I can!' said Nicholas. 'It was under that tree where we had our sandwiches.'

Then, of course, Melanie Brown remembered pushing him down into the big roots.

'Well,' said Miss Bradley, 'we certainly can't go back for him now. It would take too long and the driver won't wait. I'll phone the zoo tomorrow,

Melanie, and ask about him. Someone will find him, I'm sure. So stop crying and we'll go and see the real bears!'

But Melanie Brown's day was quite spoiled. She trailed along behind the others and hardly glanced at the big black bears or the tiny koalas. She was so tired and miserable that she fell asleep on the way home. But even asleep she could not forget her troubles. She dreamed of poor Woolly Brown Bear lying all alone under the cold night sky!

Next day, however, Miss Bradley phoned the zoo and the keeper soon found him. He made Woolly Brown Bear into a parcel with brown paper and string and posted him back to the school. Melanie Brown was *so* pleased to see him again she gave him a great big hug which nearly squashed him flat!

Melanie Brown's Exciting News

Ten o'clock in the morning was news-time. The children tidied away the paints and bricks and crayons and closed the door on the Wendy House. Then they sat in a little group with Miss Bradley to tell each other their news. Melanie Brown loved news-time when she had some news to tell, but she didn't much care for listening to other people's news. She soon got very bored.

'My Auntie's coming to stay,' Nicholas told them one morning, 'and she's going to stay the night – and she's got a baby – and I'm going to sleep in the – '

'People are *always* coming to stay with us!' said Melanie Brown, interrupting him, but Miss Bradley frowned at her and said, 'Go on Nicholas.'

But Melanie Brown's interruption had made him forget what he was going to say. He stared hopefully at the ceiling but it didn't help, so Miss Bradley said he could have another turn later if he remembered.

Then it was Susan's turn.

'I'm getting a pencil case for my birthday,' she said, 'and it's going to be a wooden one, with a lid that slides!'

She sat down again and Melanie Brown leaned across to Christopher.

'I've already got one,' she said, 'and they're no good because the lid keeps getting stuck!'

But Christopher wasn't listening. He was waving his arm furiously to catch Miss Bradley's eye.

'We'd better hear Christopher's news,' she laughed, 'before he goes off bang!'

He jumped to his feet.

'My Dad's building a garage,' he said proudly, 'and it's going to be bricks and concrete – and my Mum says he's not to walk it all into the kitchen or she'll be mad!'

While Miss Bradley was saying how clever Christopher's father was, Melanie Brown was racking her brains to try and think of some news. The trouble was nothing exciting was happening at her house just then. At last she could bear it no longer, and she put up her hand.

'Melanie?'

She stood up slowly and then stared Miss Bradley straight in the eye.

'We're going on holiday,' she said, ' – to Africa!'

There was an amazed silence.

'And when we come back my Auntie's coming to stay – and she's got hundreds of babies! – And my Mummy's got a necklace made of real diamonds! – And it's my birthday today!'

She sat down amid cries of astonishment and disbelief. Her eyes gleamed triumphantly as she looked round at the other children and then she looked at Miss Bradley. Miss Bradley seemed to be having a coughing fit, and was hiding her face in her handkerchief. Or was she laughing? Melanie Brown looked at her suspiciously. Denise put her hand up and Miss Bradley nodded to her.

'It can't be her birthday,' said Denise, 'because hers is after mine and I haven't had mine yet!'

Melanie Brown scowled but then Christopher spoke up.

'How can she be going to Africa?' he asked. 'They're coming on holiday with us, and we're going to Butlins!'

Melanie Brown began to explain that the Butlins they were going to was *in* Africa but Miss Bradley shook her head.

'Melanie was just having a game with us,' she said. 'But it certainly was exciting! But now *I* have some news for you.'

The children stared at her open-mouthed. A teacher having news? Whatever next!

'I am going to be married soon,' she told them. 'I shall still be your teacher but I shall have a new name. I shall be Mrs Collins.'

'What a funny name!' said Susan.

'I don't think it's funny,' said Melanie Brown quickly and then she added, 'Do you need any bridesmaids?'

Miss Bradley said that she didn't.

'Can I be a page-boy, then?' Melanie Brown asked hopefully, but Christopher said only boys could be page-boys. It was very disappointing.

That afternoon they had great fun, making a big fluffy sheep out of tissue paper. Melanie Brown forgot her disappointment and stuck on tissue paper as fast as she could. But then Miss Bradley said she needed someone to paint the sheep's nose and feet black.

'Me! Me!' cried everyone, but Miss Bradley could only choose one and she chose John. Then Melanie Brown lost interest in the tissue paper and went into the book corner to be miserable. She was waiting for Miss Bradley to notice her but Miss Bradley was too busy. When the sheep was finished it looked quite real and they were all very pleased with their handiwork. They cleared away the scraps of tissue paper and Miss Bradley washed the paste brushes. Melanie Brown was still sitting in the book corner and at last Miss Bradley noticed her.

'Oh, that's where you're hiding is it?' she said 'Come out and look at our sheep. I think it needs some grass to eat. Perhaps tomorrow you could draw some with a green felt-tipped pen.'

Melanie Brown cheered up at once and came out of the book corner to admire the sheep. The rest of the class were getting their hats and coats on because it was home-time. Miss Bradley looked down at Melanie Brown's hands.

'Goodness!' she said. 'Look how sticky you are! You had better wash your hands before you go home.'

The other children said 'goodbye' and hurried out. Melanie Brown didn't like being last so she rushed for the soap. Just as she took it in her hand she noticed something sparkling deep down in the plug hole of the sink.

'Miss Bradley!' she cried. 'Come quickly and see what this is!'

Miss Bradley took one look and gasped. She looked at her hand and saw that her engagement ring was missing.

'Good gracious!' she said. 'That's my ring down there! Oh, you are a clever girl to have seen it! It must have come off while I was washing the brushes! I must ask Mr Bloggs to get it up for me. He'll be here in a minute.'

When Mr Bloggs arrived he unscrewed the pipe and got the ring out. Miss Bradley was so pleased that she gave him some money to buy some tobacco. And she gave Melanie Brown six toffees from her special tin!

'And tomorrow,' said Melanie Brown triumphantly, 'I really will have something exciting to tell at news-time!'

And she was right!

Melanie Brown is Too Helpful

The school television set was not at all like the set in Melanie Brown's home. It was much bigger and stood on four legs, at one end of the hall. There were two doors at the front which were always kept locked until the teachers opened them with a small key. When it was time to watch the television the children all carried chairs into the hall and arranged them in rows.

Melanie Brown looked forward to the television programmes. One was about puppets and the other was about fire-engines and shops and animals and aeroplanes – and so many things there is no time to tell them all! As soon as they went into the hall Miss Bradley would switch the set on at the wall, and while it was warming up she would pull the curtains to shut out the light.

Now one day Melanie Brown was feeling helpful. She had given out the milk without spilling a single drop. She had found a missing piece of jigsaw, and she had cleaned the blackboard. She was still feeling particularly helpful when they went into the hall to watch the puppets. To her surprise Miss Bradley went straight over to the windows to pull the curtains, so Melanie Brown guessed at once that she had forgotten to switch the set on and without a moment's hesitation she ran across to the wall and flicked the switch! She was very pleased with herself. Four helpful things in one morning! She sat down on her chair feeling very proud and they all waited for the programme to begin.

They waited and waited – and waited! But nothing happened.

'That's funny,' said Miss Bradley. 'I wonder what's wrong. It was working before play-time. I'll have a look at it.'

She looked at the back of the set to see if the aerial was properly connected, because sometimes it worked loose. Not this time, though. She twiddled all the knobs and tried the other channels. Nothing. She looked up at the clock and frowned.

'Oh dear! We have missed the beginning.' she said. 'I had better tell Miss Grainger. Just sit quietly for a moment, children.'

Miss Grainger was the head-mistress, so they all knew it was a serious matter. They sat like mice until Miss Bradley and Miss Grainger came into the hall. Miss Grainger did all the things that Miss Bradley had done but still the television remained quite blank.

'How very odd,' said Miss Grainger. 'You say it was working perfectly before play?'

'Yes,' said Miss Bradley. 'Mrs Jones's class watched something and she left it on for us.'

'I'll give Mr Bloggs a ring,' said Miss Grainger. 'It will only take a minute or two to have a look at it. And what nice patient children you are!' she said, turning to them. 'I think Melanie Brown is one of the quietest.'

Melanie Brown beamed with delight and Miss Bradley smiled at her. Soon Mr Bloggs arrived on his bicycle with a book of instructions in his pocket. He marched into the hall and opened the book importantly. Then he glared at Miss Bradley.

'Can't we have a bit more light in here?' he asked sternly, and Miss Bradley hurried to draw back the curtains. He turned over several pages and said 'Aha!' and scratched his nose. Melanie Brown thought it was almost as much fun watching Mr Bloggs as it would have been watching the puppets!

'I think it's your power pack,' he said at last and retired behind the set. They could see his feet and legs and they could hear him breathing heavily. Then he said 'Damn!' in a loud voice.

Melanie Brown was shocked.

'He said "Damn",' she said. 'He shouldn't say that!'

'Poor Mr Bloggs,' said Miss Bradley. 'I'm sure he didn't mean it. I think he's hurt himself.'

Mr Bloggs reappeared, looking hot and flustered.

'Can't have been off long,' he grumbled. 'It's still hot!'

He looked hopefully at the screen, which remained empty.

'Why don't you thump it?' cried Christopher. 'That's what my Dad does!'

Mr Bloggs raised his hand and for one thrilling moment they thought he was going to, but he hesitated.

'Better not,' he said reluctantly, dropping his hand. He had another look in his book, then shook his head.

'Could it be something wrong with the aerial itself?' suggested Miss Bradley.

'Ah, that'll be it!' he said. 'I reckon you've hit the nail on the head! The aerial! Now that'll be a job for the aerial people, not me! I'll tell Miss Grainger to get in touch with them right away.'

They watched him go regretfully.

'Now we can't see the puppets,' wailed Denise.

'Never mind,' said Miss Bradley. 'I expect it will be mended in time for tomorrow's programme. Now, take your chairs back to the classroom. I'll just switch off the – '

She stopped in the middle of the sentence and stared at the switch. 'It's not switched on! But Mrs Jones said it was!'

She put the switch down and waited, watching the set. Music and pictures appeared and all the children clapped their hands and cheered. But Miss Bradley didn't cheer. She switched it off again and looked round. The children took one look at her face and stopped cheering.

'Did anyone touch this switch?' she asked quietly.

Melanie Brown put her hand up and Miss Bradley groaned.

'Not you again, Melanie?' she said faintly.

'I only switched it on,' said Melanie Brown, 'because you forgot.'

'I did *not* forget!' said Miss Bradley. 'I didn't need to switch it on because it was already on! You must have switched it off!'

There was a terrible silence.

'Oh well, I suppose you didn't mean it,' said Miss
Bradley. 'But I don't think Miss Grainger's going to
be too pleased about it.'

Melanie Brown thought it was very ungrateful of
Miss Bradley to talk like that and decided not to help
her ever again. She told Miss Bradley what she had
decided and Miss Bradley said, 'Is that a threat or a
promise!'

Sometimes, thought Melanie Brown, teachers could
be very difficult!

Melanie Brown and the Big Ball

Sometimes when the weather was fine, the children went into the playground with three big wire baskets. These baskets were full of exciting things. There were little square bags called bean-bags which the children threw to each other. Sometimes they balanced them on their heads or jumped around with the bean-bag held between their feet. That was really quite difficult.

There were bats, too, small cricket bats and ping-pong bats, and plenty of balls, all colours and sizes. There were skipping ropes, as well, and bamboo canes to jump over.

Melanie Brown liked the big balls best. One day, when the sun was shining, they carried the wire baskets into the playground and Melanie Brown chose a big blue ball.

'Now remember,' said Miss Bradley, 'don't throw the balls too high or too far because they might go over the fence into the lane. Try to be sensible with them.'

Melanie Brown *did* try, and she *was* sensible. She threw the big ball up a little way and caught it. She did that five times! Miss Bradley said, 'Clever girl,' because, after all, she was only five years old.

Then they changed over and tried something else.

Melanie Brown got a skipping rope out of the basket, but though she tried very hard she could not skip. It was very annoying, because Melanie liked to be good at everything. She kept trying, but it was no good. She felt cross with herself and cross with the rope, so she threw it back into the wire basket.

She took the blue ball out of the basket again, and she was so pleased to be doing something she was good at, that she threw the ball very, very high. She was quite sure she could catch it. She watched it go up and up and held out her arms for it. But it did not come down again!

The school roof was quite flat, and that is where the ball landed. Right on the edge of the roof, nearly in the gutter. Melanie Brown stared up, open-mouthed. She could just see a little bit of blue. She looked round hastily to see if Miss Bradley had noticed, but she was watching Christopher. Melanie Brown picked up the skipping-rope again and tried to skip.

'Good, Melanie,' said Miss Bradley. 'I think you'll be able to skip before long if you keep on trying.'

She cheered up at once, and began to practise and once the rope did come up over her head properly, and once or twice it went under her feet properly, and soon she forgot all about the big blue ball.

After dinner all the children went out to play and Mrs Jones went out with them to make sure no one was rough, and to look after anyone who fell over.

All the big children were out in the playground as well as Melanie Brown's class. Some of the big children were nearly eleven. Melanie Brown sat on the grass and watched two of the big boys wrestling. They rolled about on the grass, pulling and pushing and yelling at the top of their voices, and then sat up laughing, red in the face. Melanie Brown thought it was a silly game. Suddenly, one of the boys glanced up at the roof, and he saw the big blue ball.

'Mrs Jones, Mrs Jones,' he cried, 'there's a ball on the roof!'

Everyone stared up at the roof. Melanie Brown

stared too. Mrs Jones walked across the playground to get a better view.

'So there is,' she said. 'I wonder how that got up there.'

The boy who had first seen the ball got very excited.

'Please can I get it down, Mrs Jones? I saw it first.'

'Well, someone will have to get it down,' she said. 'But I don't think you can reach it.'

'Please, Mrs Jones, there's a broom round by the shed – the gardener's broom. I could knock it down with that.'

And he rushed away round the corner of the school and was soon back with the broom. He held it by its bristly end and stretched up as high as he could but the end of the handle did not quite reach the ball. So Mrs Jones told him to take the broom back again.

Then one of the big girls had an idea.

'Mrs Jones, I think there's a ladder in the shed, because Mr Bloggs had one when the gutter was overflowing.'

Mrs Jones sent her into school to ask the headmistress for the key to the shed. There *was* a ladder in there and it was just long enough to reach the gutter. So a boy went up the ladder, while Mrs Jones held it steady.

Melanie Brown held her breath as the boy reached the gutter and picked up the big blue ball. He could not hold the ball while he climbed down, so he threw it down into the playground.

And a very odd thing happened. The ball bounced on the ground and then bounced up and hit Melanie

Brown in the tummy! She fell over backwards, and sat there on the ground staring at the ball. It was just as though the ball knew that she had thrown it up there and was punishing her!

All the children laughed, but one of the big girls helped her up again and brushed her skirt down.

When the ladder was put back in the shed again, Mrs Jones came over to her.

'Poor Melanie,' she said. 'That was bad luck, wasn't it? Never mind, you're not hurt, are you?'

Melanie Brown shook her head slowly. She did not answer because she was thinking. Next time they took out the wire baskets she would leave the balls well alone and learn to skip!

Melanie Brown's Birthday Party

Melanie Brown could be very awkward at times and one of the times was when she was planning her birthday party.

'I want everyone in the whole school to come,' she told her mother hopefully.

'Don't be silly, dear,' said Mrs Brown.

'Well, the whole class, then.'

'No, Melanie!' said her mother patiently. 'You know we couldn't possibly fit all those children in. Do be sensible.'

Melanie Brown thought about it.

'Well then,' she said, 'I want Mr Bloggs to come because he rescued me when I was up the tree, and I want the milkman to come – '

'If you don't stop being silly,' said Mrs Brown, 'no one will come because you won't have a party! Just think of five of your friends.'

So Melanie Brown decided to ask Christopher, Denise, Paula, Nicholas and John. Mrs Brown bought a packet of invitation cards and they sent one each to the five children and they all said they could come. Mrs Brown made a birthday cake with 'MELANIE' on it in pink icing, and bought some pink slippers to match Melanie Brown's best pink dress. Melanie

Brown was so excited that she counted the days to the party! But then – oh dear! She quarrelled with her five friends! This is how it happened.

It was play-time and the six children were playing together on the grass.

'We'll play witches,' said Melanie Brown, 'and that bush can be the witch's house and you are all walking past – '

'It could be a gingerbread house!' said Paula. 'Like the one in *Hansel and Gretel*.'

'All right, then, a gingerbread house,' said Melanie Brown, 'and you are all walking past – '

'And we all eat the house!' cried Nicholas and he began to make loud eating noises. Melanie Brown frowned at him severely.

'Don't keep interrupting,' she said. 'I have to say what we do because it's my game.'

'It's not your game!' said Paula.

'It is!' cried Melanie Brown. 'I thought of it!'

'But I thought of the gingerbread house – '

'It doesn't matter whose game it is,' said John. 'Let's get on with it. Who's going to be the witch?'

'I am!' cried the three girls together.

John laughed. 'We can't have three witches!' he said.

'I should be the witch,' said Melanie Brown, 'because I'm the oldest.'

'You're not!' said Christopher. 'I'm the oldest.'

'Oh,' said Melanie Brown, 'then I should be the witch because I'm the youngest!'

'You're not the youngest,' said Denise.

Then they began to argue and Melanie Brown got crosser and crosser.

'If you don't let me be the witch then I won't let you come to my party!' she shouted.

'Don't want to come to your silly old party!' said Denise. 'So there!'

Melanie Brown was so shocked she hardly knew what to say.

'You're all horrible!' she said, nearly bursting into tears. 'I hate you and you're not coming to my party!'

And she ran away to find a corner to cry in.

But none of the children told their mothers about the quarrel – not even Melanie Brown. Instead she found the packet of invitation cards and filled in the seven cards that were left with different names. Next

day she gave them out to the seven children and they took them home to show their mothers. While all this was happening Mrs Brown was busy buying things for the party. She bought six crackers and six funny hats and she made six jellies. By the time Friday came round Melanie Brown had got over her temper and she told her five best friends that they *could* come after all! So altogether she had invited twelve children but Mrs Brown didn't know that!

Saturday afternoon came at last and Melanie Brown put on her pink dress and the pink slippers and felt very fine. Paula arrived and then John, quickly followed by Christopher, Nicholas and Denise. They each gave her a present and she was busily unwrapping them when the door bell rang again.

'I'll see who it is,' said Grandmother, who had also come to the party. Jennifer stood on the step with her mother.

'I do hope we're not too early,' said Jennifer's mother.

Grandmother shook her head and led Jennifer into the lounge to join the others. Mrs Brown looked rather puzzled but before she could say anything the bell

rang again! This time Mr Brown went to answer it while Mrs Brown and Grandmother stared at each other in dismay.

When all twelve children had arrived the three grown-ups left them opening presents and rushed into the kitchen to wonder what to do!

'Isn't it awful!' wailed Mrs Brown. 'All those children! We haven't enough chairs – or plates – or funny hats. Everything will be spoiled! I just can't understand how it's happened.'

It was a good thing Grandmother was there because she was very wise. She sorted things out in no time. Father went to the nearest shop for some cardboard cups and plates. Mother took the children into the garden for some party games and Grandmother made some more sandwiches. The six jellies went into the fridge for another day and the crackers and funny hats went into the cupboard to wait for Christmas.

Tea was a picnic in the garden and everyone agreed it was much more fun than an ordinary tea. After tea they played some more games until it was time to go home.

When Mrs Brown tucked Melanie Brown into bed that night she asked her how it was that so many children came to the party, and Melanie Brown told her.

'But it was so much fun!' she said. 'Can I ask them all again next year?'

Mrs Brown laughed. 'I'll think about it,' she said.

PART THREE

for
AILSA

Melanie Brown and the Jar of Sweets

Melanie Brown's sixth birthday came and went and she was just as naughty as ever! It wasn't that she always meant to be naughty – sometimes she did mean to, but sometimes things just happened to her. She went to the village school and had a nice teacher whose name was Miss Bradley, and a nice boyfriend whose name was Christopher.

Every year, during the summer, Melanie Brown's school had a fête to collect money for the school fund. All the mothers made things to sell – cakes for the cake stall and toys for the toy stall. There were competitions and games and everyone enjoyed it tremendously.

'I like the guessing things best,' said Christopher. 'Last year my auntie guessed how heavy the cake was and so they gave it to her and it had pink icing on it and we all had a piece.'

Melanie Brown for once said nothing because she had missed the fête altogether, being in bed with the measles, but she didn't intend to miss it again.

'I'll make a doll for the toy stall,' said Grandmother when Melanie Brown told her about the fete. And she made a rag doll with button eyes and brown wool plaits. Her dress was red with white spots and there was a bonnet to match. Melanie Brown was very proud of her clever grandmother.

'But what can *I* do?' she wailed, for the twentieth time. Mrs Brown thought hard.

'I know,' she said at last. 'We'll fill a big glass jar with sweets and people can try to guess how many sweets there are. What about that?'

Melanie Brown liked the idea, so that was quickly settled.

The morning of the fête was rather dull and cloudy, but Mr Bloggs, the caretaker, said the wind was in the wrong direction for rain, so they went ahead with their plans to have most of the stalls outside in the playground. Mr Bloggs knew about such matters and he was always right. At three o'clock the visitors started to arrive and Melanie Brown's inside felt all fluttery because she was nervous.

'Now remember, Melanie,' said her mother. 'Don't tell anyone – not even Christopher – how many sweets there are in the jar. It has to be a secret until the end of the afternoon.'

(They had counted the sweets and there were fifty-three!)

Melanie Brown sat on a chair with the jar on another chair beside her. Next to the jar was one of Mr Bloggs's empty tobacco tins for the money. She also had a notebook and pencil.

She didn't have to wait long before Michael came up to her with a penny. Michael was a new boy and he was only five.

'What do I have to do?' he asked.

She told him and he gave her the penny. He shut his eyes tightly – and then opened them again.

'Don't know,' he said.

'Try and guess,' said Melanie Brown patiently, so he shut his eyes again. When he opened them again he said, 'I know! Dolly Mixtures!'

She stared at him and then at the sweets, which were boiled sweets.

'You don't have to guess *what* they are,' she told him. 'You have to guess *how many* there are. Anyone can see they're not Dolly Mixtures. Have another go.'

He shut his eyes for a third time and then said, 'Don't know, and can I have my penny back now?'

Melanie Brown took a deep breath.

'No you can't!' she said severely. 'Now just say a number.'

'Ten,' said Michael.

'Wrong!' cried Melanie Brown triumphantly. 'There are fifty-three, so there!'

He looked at her silently for a moment, then he said, 'I don't believe you.'

It was a good thing he was only five, because for a few seconds Melanie Brown had a strong desire to punch him, but instead she took the lid off the jar and tipped the sweets on to the chair.

'Look,' she said. 'I'll show you. I'll count them.'

One at a time she popped the sweets back into the jar.

'. . . eleven, twelve, thirteen . . .'

Michael watched for a moment, then he lost interest and wandered away. Melanie Brown struggled on. '. . . fifty-one, fifty-two, fifty-three!' There you are! Fifty-three!'

But Michael was nowhere to be seen. Muttering darkly, she screwed the lid back on the jar just as her mother came back to see how she was getting on.

'Are you managing Melanie?' she asked. 'Or shall I take over now and you can go off with your friends?'

'I'm managing,' said Melanie Brown and she really thought she was, but as soon as her mother had gone she had a terrible thought. She had told Michael how many sweets there were in the jar and it was supposed to be a secret! Before she could decide what to do about it a lady came along, gave her a penny, and looked carefully at the jar of sweets.

'I guess sixty-one,' she said and wrote her name in the notebook with a '61' after it. Then Christopher guessed a hundred and Denise guessed twenty-seven, but all the time the money was dropping into the tin Melanie Brown was worrying about telling Michael the secret. Suddenly she had an idea. When no one was looking she opened the jar, took out a sweet, and put it into her mouth. Now there were only fifty-two sweets in the jar.

'And I told Michael fifty-three,' she told herself, 'so that's all right.'

At the end of the afternoon, when the winners of the competitions were announced, Mrs Brown called out fifty-three as the number of sweets in the jar, because she didn't know Melanie Brown had eaten one. Mr Bloggs had guessed fifty-three, so he won the sweets. Melanie Brown wondered what would happen if he decided to count them, but he said he was on a diet and he gave them all away to the children. So Melanie Brown had another one.

It must have been her lucky day!

Melanie Brown's Bad Day

As soon as Melanie Brown got out of bed her mother knew it was going to be one of those days! First Melanie Brown put her socks on inside out and then she pretended she couldn't fasten the buckle on her sandal. She left half her boiled egg, and put so much marmalade on her toast that while she was eating one side of it all the marmalade fell off the other side on to the clean tablecloth.

Melanie was sorry the day was going so badly, but when she arrived at school things took a turn for the better.

'Don't take off your coat,' Denise told her, 'and don't change your shoes, because we're going for a walk.'

'That's right,' said Miss Bradley. 'We'll go across the fields as far as the stream and see what we can see.'

'I expect we'll see some cows,' said John, because they knew Miss Bradley was not very fond of cows.

'Cows don't hurt you,' said Melanie Brown quickly in case Miss Bradley changed her mind.

'Wild ones do!' said John, but since no one had ever seen a wild cow they took no notice and rushed to line up at the door.

The sun was shining as they set off. They walked quietly along the lane and through the churchyard, but once into the field on the other side they were free to run and shout for a few minutes.

'And now we'll be very quiet,' said Miss Bradley, 'and close our eyes and listen.'

They all concentrated very hard and heard a train, a man sawing wood, a dog barking – and Melanie Brown whispering when she should have been listening!

But the stream was the most exciting part of the walk. It was not very wide and not very deep, but it was dark and green with mysterious weeds, and the banks were sprinkled with forget-me-nots and watermint. The children stood along the edge looking hopefully for fish. Miss Bradley had brought a large jam-jar and a net in case they saw anything interesting. They took it in turn to dip the net into the water and examine the 'catch'. Christopher found a water-snail and Susan found a small black wriggly thing. No one knew what it was, but they put it in the jar with some water and some weed.

'My turn,' said Melanie Brown, but it wasn't, so she hopped and fidgeted along the edge of the stream, waiting impatiently until it was.

'Be careful, Melanie!' Miss Bradley warned her. 'Don't stand too close to the edge. We don't want to have to fish *you* out with the net!'

'I never fall in,' Melanie Brown told Christopher, who was trying to undo a knot in his lace so that he could take his shoes off and dangle his feet in the water when Miss Bradley wasn't looking.

At last it was Melanie Brown's turn and she determined to find something more interesting than any of the others had found. She swished the net backwards and forwards at a tremendous speed, leaning farther and farther over the water. Miss Bradley was busy with Michael, who had stung himself on a nettle, and there was no one to say 'Be careful' so of course Melanie Brown managed to overbalance and one leg went into the water – plop! She gave a loud scream as her foot began to sink into the mud at the bottom of the stream. She threw up her arms and the net flew out of her hand and began to float away downstream.

The rest of the class jumped up and down shouting, 'Help! Help!' and 'Melanie Brown's drowning!' and unhelpful things like that. Denise told Susan to run back to school and fetch a long rope so that they could pull her out, but Susan didn't want to miss anything so she didn't go. John stood on one leg and gave a demonstration of how to swim the breast stroke, but since Melanie Brown only had one leg in the water that wasn't very helpful either, and she was thankful when at last Miss Bradley arrived to pull her out.

Her foot came out with a loud squelching noise and everyone cheered – until they saw that her sandal was missing!

'Oh no!' said Miss Bradley, dismayed. 'It must have

come off in the mud.'

They all stared down at the water, which was no longer dark and green but a pale coffee colour where the mud had been stirred up. Melanie Brown wondered what her mother was going to say when she hopped home with only one sandal, but Miss Bradley, looking rather thundery, was rolling up her sleeve. A hush descended as the children watched her. She had to lie down sideways along the edge of the stream and reach deep into the water, which came way up past her elbow. After a moment or two there was another 'squelch' and Melanie Brown's sandal reappeared.

They washed the muddy sock and sandal in the clearer water upstream and Christopher offered to carry them.

'But how am I going to get back to school?' asked Melanie Brown. 'Someone will have to give me a piggy-back.'

She stared hard at Miss Bradley as she said this, but the teacher had suddenly gone deaf in that ear and took no notice.

'You'll have to hop,' said Susan. 'It's quite easy. Kangaroos do it all the time.'

'But they hop with both legs,' said Melanie Brown. 'And anyway I'm not a kangaroo. I'm a girl.'

'And a very naughty girl at that!' said Miss Bradley crossly. 'If you had been careful like the others it would never have happened. Now you will have to walk back to school with one foot bare or wear your wet sock and sandal. Which is it to be?'

Melanie Brown decided to wear her wet sock and

sandal, and she walked back to school in gloomy silence. At bedtime she had a blister on her heel.

'How did you get that?' her mother asked her.

When Melanie Brown explained, Mrs Brown said, 'That's what comes of not doing what you're told,' and Mr Brown said that in his opinion Miss Bradley would be grey before she was thirty.

Melanie Brown and the Flood

Would you believe it could rain every day for a whole week? Well, it did! It seemed as though it would never stop raining. The puddles in the lane got bigger and bigger and deeper and deeper. The children found it all great fun, but Mr Bloggs hated the rain because he was the caretaker. Every morning he put sheets of newspaper down on the classroom floor just inside the door so that mud from the children's boots didn't tread all over the room.

Melanie Brown loved the rain. She wrote a story about it.

'It is raining. It rained yesterday. It might rain again tomorrow. Soon it will be a flood. Mr Bloggs grumbles about the rain and he worries about the mud. He worries all the time.'

Then she drew a picture of Mr Bloggs standing on six blades of grass with very large drops of rain falling all around him. She got rather carried away with the raindrops and some of them were nearly as big as Mr Bloggs's head! She took the picture out to show Miss Bradley.

'That's Mr Bloggs worrying,' she said.

'He's got something to worry about!' laughed Miss

Bradley. 'One of those raindrops would just about finish him off!'

But she liked the picture very much indeed and she held it up for the rest of the class to see. Then Melanie Brown read out the story.

'Will there really be a flood?' Denise asked nervously.

'Oh no, I don't think so,' said Miss Bradley – but she was wrong!

That night the pond in the lane was so full of water it overflowed, and the water spread out across the grass. It reached the hedge and trickled through into the lane. By morning the lane was full of muddy brown water. When the children arrived for school they could hardly believe their eyes. They crowded up to the edge of the water, pushing and shouting and dipping the toes of their shoes and boots into it. Of course Melanie Brown dipped her shoe in too far and the cold water crept in at the lace holes and made her sock feel nasty. While she was wondering whom to blame for this Miss Bradley drove up in her car and got out to see what was going on.

'It's a flood!' they told her. 'A real flood!'

'So it is!' she said, amazed. 'Melanie Brown was right. I wonder how deep it is. I think I'll try and drive through to the car park.'

'Some of us could come with you,' said Christopher hopefully, but Miss Bradley thought not.

'In case I get stuck halfway,' she said.

So they watched her get back into the car and start up the engine. Slowly, slowly the car moved through

the water until it came halfway up the wheels.

'I do hope she can swim,' said Denise.

'I can,' said Melanie Brown and she began to whirl her arms round and round above her head.

'That's not how you swim,' said John. 'You look more like a helicopter!'

Melanie Brown was just wondering whether or not to push him into the water when a loud cheer went up. Miss Bradley was safely across to the other side. She drove into the car park and came out a few moments later with Mr Bloggs. They stood wondering what to do next. Suddenly Melanie Brown had a clever idea.

'If we had some chairs in the water we could walk across them like stepping-stones,' she said.

Miss Bradley thought they should try it out, and she and Mr Bloggs went into school and came out again with some chairs from the top class. Mr Bloggs was wearing high boots called waders, so he was able to carry the chairs and arrange them in a line in the water. Because they were top-class chairs the seats were just high enough to be above the water. While Miss Bradley and Mr Bloggs went back for more chairs Melanie Brown told all the children to make a line behind her, ready for the walk across the water, and because it was all her idea they did what they were told without arguing.

When at last the row of chairs reached from one side of the water to the other Mr Bloggs waded across and helped Melanie Brown up on to the first chair. Everyone held their breath, because the chairs weren't very steady and wobbled when she stepped on to them, but with Mr Bloggs holding her hand she made her way safely to the other side. There was another great cheer as she turned to wave triumphantly and then it was time for the next child to cross. Melanie Brown thought it was the most exciting day of her whole life!

By the time the other teachers arrived most of the children were across, and the rest were taken across by car to hurry things up. They thought that was very exciting, too.

After such an extraordinary start to the day the children found it very hard to settle down to their work. They were hoping that the flood would still be there when it was time to go home, but they were disappointed. By dinner-time the level of the water had dropped a little and by afternoon play-time the men from the council had been to unblock the drains and help the water to seep away even faster.

'Never mind,' said Miss Bradley. 'It was fun while it lasted.'

As Melanie Brown and Christopher walked home from school later that day he asked her how she had known that there was going to be a flood, but she merely smiled mysteriously and said nothing.

Melanie Brown Goes for a Ride

One day, at News Time, Miss Bradley said, 'Do you remember last year's outing when we went to the zoo?' and all the children started talking at once because they did remember.

'Well,' she said, when they had quietened down, 'this year we are going somewhere different. We are going to visit a beautiful house which was once the home of a king. There are wonderful things to see in the house and there is a beautiful garden with peacocks and flamingoes and – '

'I bet it's Buckingham Palace!' cried Susan and they all thought it was, but it wasn't.

'The house is called Aubrey Grange,' Miss Bradley told them, 'and we shall – '

Melanie Brown jumped to her feet.

'I've been there! I've been there!' she shouted. 'I went with my Auntie Pat and Uncle Mike and we had tea in the tea-room and I had a ham sandwich and my uncle said we needed a microscope to see the ham and I had Coca-Cola and there was a little train. Are we going on the train?'

The children looked hopefully at Miss Bradley, but she shook her head.

'I'm afraid we won't have time,' she said, 'but there is a big dolls' house and suits of armour in the house – '

'But the train is the best thing!' Melanie Brown told her earnestly. 'Why won't we have time? It goes through a tunnel and over a bridge and the carriages don't have any roofs and there's a driver. Why can't we go on it?'

Miss Bradley sighed.

'I've told you,' she said. 'I don't think we'll have time.'

Melanie Brown sat down as suddenly as she had jumped up, and no one could think of anything to say, until Miss Bradley asked Melanie Brown to tell the children about the peacocks and flamingoes. Melanie Brown stood up reluctantly.

'They're birds,' she said. 'The flamingoes are pink and the peacocks are brown – and you can see them from the train as you're going along but they aren't scared of the train because – '

'Melanie!' said Miss Bradley quickly. 'That's quite enough about the train!'

But it was too late. The children could think of nothing else and Melanie Brown was quite certain that without the train-ride the outing would be a complete disaster.

She talked about the train whenever she could. She talked about it at News Time and she brought a photograph which her Uncle Mike had taken and which showed Melanie Brown and her Auntie Pat sitting in the train.

'And the ride only costs five pence,' she added.

She painted a big picture of the train and pinned it to the wall, and she made a train out of plasticine and gave it a track made of matchsticks. She even made up a song about a train which went out in the rain and fell down a drain – and that was when Miss Bradley finally admitted defeat. She asked the Head Mistress if she could take the children on the train and the Head Mistress said, 'Yes.'

'So we *can* go on the train,' Miss Bradley told them, 'but you will each have to bring another five pence to pay for it, so remember to ask your mothers.'

The day of the outing was bright and sunny and the children had a wonderful time. They walked round the house, which was very grand indeed, and saw the bed which the king used to sleep in. They saw the dolls' house which belonged to the little princesses and a needlework box which belonged to the queen. Outside in the gardens they saw the peacocks and flamingoes and a big fountain. Miss Bradley took some photographs and then they had a picnic lunch on the grass.

Then, at last, it was time for the train-ride. The train was waiting for them and there were no other passengers, because Miss Bradley had booked the whole train. They scrambled up into the little coaches and waited impatiently for the driver, who was talking to another man. While they waited they waved to each other across the coaches. Miss Bradley sat at the end of the train so that she could keep an eye on them all.

'Now remember what I told you,' she said. 'Don't lean out too far or you might fall out. We don't want to lose anyone!'

Suddenly the driver said, 'Cheerio' to his friend and climbed into his seat. There was a loud hissing from the engine, three quick 'toots' – and they were off. It was every bit as thrilling as Melanie Brown had promised. The engine gathered speed and they made their way through the grounds of Aubrey Grange, in and out of the trees and over the bridge. Melanie Brown was sitting with her back to the engine and she waved happily to Miss Bradley at the other end of the train.

'Right, you children,' shouted the engine driver, 'keep your heads down! We're coming to the tunnel!'

The engine was making so much noise that Melanie Brown felt quite sure no one could hear him. She stood up and began to shout at the top of her voice.

'Keep your heads down, everybody! Keep your heads down! We're coming to the tunnel!'

She was so busy telling the others to keep their heads down that she quite forgot about her own head. Miss Bradley waved frantically to her and the driver put on the brakes, but he couldn't stop the train in time.

The edge of the tunnel caught Melanie Brown's head and gave her a bang that knocked her over. It hurt so much that she thought it had knocked her head right off! The driver stopped the train and picked her up. Miss Bradley came running along beside the train to see if she was still in one piece.

'You'll have a nice big bump there soon!' the driver told Melanie Brown, and he told Miss Bradley she was lucky to have got off so lightly. Miss Bradley thought

so too. Melanie Brown blinked back the tears and said nothing, but she sat on Miss Bradley's lap on the coach going home, feeling very sorry for herself.

When Mr Brown met her off the coach Miss Bradley told him what had happened.

'Don't worry,' he said cheerfully. 'Our Melanie's got a head like a brick! She'll survive.'

'Poor Melanie,' said Miss Bradley. 'She was so determined to go on that train.'

'Do you wish you hadn't?' asked Denise.

Melanie Brown shook her aching head.

'Of course I don't,' she said firmly. 'It was the best bit of the whole day!'

And do you know, she really meant it!

Melanie Brown and the Pets' Service

One evening Melanie Brown fixed her mother with a very stern look.

'We all have to take a pet to school on Friday,' she said, 'or we shall get into dreadful trouble – '

Mrs Brown popped some cakes into the oven.

'I'm sure Miss Bradley didn't put it quite like that,' she laughed.

'So you'll have to buy me a pet,' Melanie Brown went on, ignoring the interruption. 'Susan is taking Ted, her tortoise, and Andrew is taking a mouse in a cage, and I want to take something, because we're going to sing hymns about animals.'

Mrs Brown thought about it.

'Mrs Stevens might let you take Bimbo,' she suggested. Mrs Stevens was the lady next door and Bimbo was a very old poodle. Melanie Brown shook her head.

'I want to take something interesting,' she said, 'like an elephant.'

'You'd never get it through the school door,' said her mother, but Melanie Brown thought a baby one would just about go through.

'Or it could stand outside and listen through the window,' she said hopefully.

Mrs Brown could see it was going to be one of those difficult conversations, so she said, 'Ask your father when he comes home.'

So Melanie Brown asked him.

'What about a budgie?' he suggested. 'Auntie Pat might let you take hers.'

'Someone in the top class is bringing one,' she said. 'We don't want to be crowded out with them.'

'Two budgies aren't exactly a crowd,' said her father, but Melanie Brown stared at her shoe and wouldn't talk about it.

'A snake, then,' said Mr Brown. 'One of my mates at work has a grass-snake in a – '

'I don't like snakes!' said Melanie Brown hurriedly. 'They're all thin – and they've got no legs.'

'What do you expect?' said her father. 'Who ever heard of a fat snake with legs?'

But it was no good. None of his ideas pleased her and she went to bed feeling very grieved indeed.

When Friday morning came Melanie Brown still hadn't got a pet. She set off for school as late as she could and dawdled along the road so that she wouldn't meet any of her friends with their pets. School Lane was deserted. She was passing Mrs Berry's cottage when she saw her big ginger cat, whose name was Tiger, sitting on the window-sill blinking sleepily in the early morning sunshine. She looked at it thoughtfully for a moment, then tiptoed along the garden path.

'Hullo, nice cat,' she said softly. 'Nice old Tiger, aren't you?'

To her surprise the cat stood up and rubbed its head against her shoulder.

'Like to come to a Pets' Service?' she asked coaxingly, glancing back towards the lane to see if anyone was around. 'It's hymns and prayers and things.'

There was no one in sight, so Melanie Brown picked up the cat and carried him out of the garden and along the lane to school. She could hear the children beginning to sing a hymn about animals, so she ran through the empty classroom and into the hall. She didn't notice a small cage on the floor in front of Andrew and nearly tripped over it.

'Melanie Brown's frightening my mouse!' cried
Andrew loudly.

She turned round to say, 'I'm not!' and stepped on
Ted, the tortoise.

'Look where you're going, Melanie!' hissed Susan.
'You kicked Ted!'

'I didn't mean to,' she said. 'It's Andrew's fault.
He shouldn't leave his mouse on – '

The piano stopped suddenly as Miss Bradley turned
round to see what all the fuss was about.

'Are you settled now, Melanie?' she asked
hopefully.

Melanie Brown nodded.

Miss Bradley smiled at her. 'I like your cat,' she said. 'It's a lovely colour.'

And she turned back to the piano and began to play the third verse. Melanie Brown sang as loudly as she could to make up for missing the first two verses. As soon as she started to sing Tiger put his ears back and wriggled in her arms and swished his tail from side to side. Melanie Brown held him a bit tighter.

'Mioaw!' said Tiger plaintively and wriggled harder than ever. Poor Melanie Brown began to feel flustered and started to sing verse five instead of verse four, and some of the children laughed.

'MIOAW!' cried Tiger again and Miss Granger walked across to Melanie Brown.

'I think you are holding your cat too tightly, dear,' she whispered. 'He doesn't like it.'

Melanie Brown loosened her hold and Tiger wriggled free, scratching her arm as he did so, and disappeared through the hall door at great speed.

'Ouch!' shrieked Melanie Brown. 'Now look what's happened! It's all your fault!' And she rushed after the cat, who by this time was halfway across the playground, heading for home. She ran straight into Mr Bloggs and knocked all the breath out of him.

'Steady on!' he said. 'What's the hurry? School on fire or something?'

She gazed across the empty playground without answering.

'How's the Pets' Service going?' said Mr Bloggs. 'Miss Granger did say I could bring my cat, but she's getting old now and looks a bit peaky this morning.'

Melanie Brown sucked the scratch on her arm.

'Cats don't like music,' she said shortly.

'Don't they now? Well, I didn't know that,' he said.

'And I don't like cats!' said Melanie Brown. 'Or dogs – or mice or tortoises.'

'Is that so?' said Mr Bloggs, hiding a smile.

'I just don't like pets,' she said. 'They're dangerous!'

And she decided to play in the Wendy House until the Pets' Service was over.

Melanie Brown and the Robot

Melanie Brown was making a robot. The body was an empty cornflakes packet covered with white paper and the legs were two cardboard tubes. She wanted him to be a standing-up robot, but he was top-heavy and kept falling over. So she moved his legs and stuck them on at the front and made him sit down instead. His eyes were two plastic bottle-tops and his nose was part of an egg-box. She was adding a piece of curly wire to the top of his head when Denise arrived with her little brother.

'This is my little brother,' she said, 'and what's that wire for?'

'It's an aerial,' said Melanie Brown.

'Robots don't have aerials,' said Denise.

'This one does.'

Denise wanted to know how the robot was turned on and off, and they both thought about it.

'I want to go home,' said Denise's little brother.

'I think he'll have to have a switch at the back,' said Melanie Brown. So they turned the robot round and she stuck on a small piece of card for the switch and wrote ON–OFF with a felt-tipped pen.

'I want to go home,' said Denise's little brother.

'You'd better take him home,' said Melanie Brown, writing the numbers 1 to 10 on the robot's back. She added a red pointer and made it point to number 7.

'If that pointer points to number 10,' she said, 'he's overheating.'

'I can't take him home,' said Denise. 'He's starting school today because he's nearly five and his name's Brian.'

Melanie Brown looked at him with interest. He was small, with ginger hair, brown eyes and freckles.

'Isn't he nice,' she said. 'I keep asking for a little brother but they keep saying, "We'll see," and, "One day . . ." '

'He's a bit of a nuisance,' said Denise. 'When he was a baby he kept on crying and when he got bigger he scribbled in my best books.'

Miss Bradley came over to admire the robot and they all watched Melanie Brown fix a pipe cleaner on to each side for his arms. Then Miss Bradley took Brian to the sand-tray and made him a big sand-pie, but he still looked very unhappy. Denise showed him the bricks and the Wendy House, but *still* he wanted to go home!

'I told you he was a nuisance,' said Denise, as Melanie Brown painted a big mouth on the robot. 'And robots can't talk.'

'They can so!' said Melanie Brown cheerfully. 'They don't move their mouths but the voice comes out . . . There! He's finished!' She put him on the window-sill to dry and turned her attention to poor little Brian, who looked as though he was going to cry.

'I'll look after him for you,' said Melanie Brown rashly and Denise retired to the Wendy House before she could change her mind.

'Would you like me to tell you a story, Brian?' she said. 'About the three bears?'

Two big tears rolled down Brian's cheeks. Melanie Brown wiped them away with her handkerchief.

'Once upon a time there were three bears and they lived in a little cottage. There was Father Bear, Mother Bear and – '

Two more big tears rolled down his face. Melanie Brown gave him a little hug, but he only cried louder and louder. Dismayed, she looked around – and noticed her robot.

'Look, Brian,' she said. 'Look at this robot. Isn't he funny! Look at his funny old nose – and his funny old eyes.'

Brian stopped crying. He looked at the robot – and began to laugh! Melanie Brown beamed at him.

'Would you like to hold him?' she asked. Brian took the robot and laughed again.

'Well done, Melanie,' said Miss Bradley. 'I see you've managed to cheer Brian up.'

Brian smiled at her.

'That girl gave me this robot,' he said. 'She *gave* it to me.'

Miss Bradley looked at Melanie Brown.

'I didn't!' she said. 'I only said he could hold it.'

But Brian was telling everyone.

'That girl gave me this robot.'

'I did not!' she protested. 'I only – '

'Look at his funny old nose!' said Brian.

He gave the nose a tweak – and it fell off! Melanie Brown closed her eyes. She simply couldn't bear to look.

'Shall I explain to him, Melanie?' Miss Bradley asked her.

Melanie Brown opened her eyes and saw Brian with the robot. Christopher was gluing the nose on again for him. She shook her head.

'It doesn't matter,' she said. 'He can keep it. I'll make another one tomorrow.'

But she thought that next time she would ask for a little sister instead!

Melanie Brown is a Server

Melanie Brown always looked forward to dinner-time at school. The children ate their dinner in the hall and eight children sat at each table. Two of these children had to be servers, and that meant asking the others how many potatoes they wanted and if they liked peas and interesting things like that. It was a very important job and Melanie Brown desperately wanted to be a server. Unfortunately the servers were supposed to be at least eight years old before they were sensible enough to do the job properly.

'But I'm nearly eight,' Melanie Brown insisted one day when Mrs Green was trying to choose a server. Mrs Green came to school every day to help with the dinners.

'Nearly eight?' said Mrs Green. 'Surely not. You're not even nearly seven.'

'But I'm taller than Lindie and she's eight,' said Melanie Brown, 'and I'm as clever as eight.'

'That still doesn't make you eight, does it?' said Mrs Green, who was always very busy and could never spare the time to argue with Melanie Brown. She chose a girl called Fiona who was ten and a boy called Nigel who was nine. Melanie Brown sat back in her chair looking sulky while Fiona and Nigel started to serve the food. It was fish and chips, which was one of her favourites.

'Is that enough chips for you, Melanie,' asked Fiona, 'or would you like some more?'

'I don't want any chips,' said Melanie Brown in a loud voice, 'and I don't want any fish!'

And she tipped her chair back as far as she could without falling over.

'Why don't you want any?' said Fiona. 'And sit up properly or Mrs Green will be after you.'

They were not allowed to tip back the chairs because if they did there was not enough room for people to walk between the tables.

'Don't care!' said Melanie Brown, but she decided to sit forward again. Then she began to fiddle with her knife and fork, pretending the knife was a saw and trying to saw the fork in half, making loud sawing noises – 'Eeh-aw, eeh-aw, eeh-aw!'

'Whatever are you doing, Melanie,' said Mrs Green, 'and why aren't you eating any dinner? I thought you liked fish and chips.'

'It's just because she can't be a server,' said John. 'Can I have some more chips if she doesn't want any?'

'No, you can't,' said Melanie Brown quickly, 'because I *do* want some, so there!'

Fiona put some fish on to her plate next to the chips and Melanie Brown began to sprinkle vinegar over the chips. She sprinkled and sprinkled and sprinkled and sprinkled and the chips got wetter and wetter and wetter.

'I think you've got enough vinegar on those chips,' said Mrs Green. 'They can't swim, you know!'

The thought of the chips swimming around in the vinegar was so funny that all the children hooted with laughter. Even Melanie Brown had to laugh and she forgot about being difficult until later on when they were eating the pudding, which was sponge and jam sauce. Fiona spilt some jam on to the table and Melanie Brown was out of her chair in a flash.

'I'll get the cloth!' she shouted and was halfway down the hall before Mrs Green appeared from nowhere and led her back to her chair. Melanie Brown was so cross that she put her tongue out at Nigel when he went to get the cloth. Then she swung her legs up and kicked the table from underneath so that all the plates and spoons rattled, and it was Mrs Green's turn to get cross.

'If I have to speak to you again, Melanie, you will have to finish your pudding in one of the classrooms, all on your own,' she said. 'You are being really tiresome today!' Before Melanie Brown could think of an answer to this Nigel interrupted.

'Mrs Green! I think one of the fish-bones has stuck in my throat. I can feel it when I swallow.'

'Poor old Nigel,' said Mrs Green. 'Let's see if we can wash it down with some water. Don't worry, dear.' And they went out of the hall to the cloakroom.

They were still out there when it was time to clear away the plates.

'*Please* let me help you,' begged Melanie Brown. Fiona hesitated – then she said, 'Well, only if we hurry up and get it done before Mrs Green comes back.'

Melanie Brown was delighted. Humming happily, she collected the plates and scraped the crumbs together. Then she piled them one on top of another.

'Not so many at once,' Fiona told her. 'You take four and I'll – '

'I can carry them! I know how to do it!' said Melanie Brown impatiently. 'Don't keep telling me!'

Determined to impress all her friends, she picked up the pile of plates and staggered away down the hall towards the trolley at the far end, and they all stopped eating to watch. Somehow she managed it! She put the pile of plates on the trolley and turned to rush

back to Fiona who was following with the spoons and the sauce-jug.

'I did it! I – '

But she was so excited she didn't look where she was going, and ran straight into a server from another table who was also carrying a pile of plates.

CRASH!

The four plates hit the floor and smashed into pieces. Everyone went very quiet suddenly, and Mrs Green and Nigel came back into the hall . . .

It was the very worst moment of Melanie Brown's life!

'Never mind,' said Christopher. 'When you're eight you'll be able to do it properly.'

Melanie Brown looked at him in amazement.

'I don't want to be a server any more,' she said, 'It's so boring!'

Melanie Brown and the Sack Race

Melanie Brown took a large bite of fruit cake and started to tell her mother and father all about Sports Day.

'I can't understand a word you're saying, Melanie,' said her mother. 'You can't talk properly with a mouthful of cake.'

Melanie Brown was just explaining how she could when a currant went down the wrong way and made her choke, and Mr Brown had to pat her back. When she had swallowed the cake she said, 'It's going to be Sports Day and you'll have to come because we're having races and I'm going to win them all.'

'All of them?' said Mr Brown. 'Are you sure?'

'Quite sure,' said Melanie Brown, but of course it wasn't quite as simple as that.

They had to practise for the races, and all the other children seemed to think that they were going to win and not Melanie Brown. They practised the skipping race, and Melanie Brown got tangled up in the rope and had to stop and untangle it.

'Never mind, dear. Just carry on,' said Miss Bradley, but she didn't. She folded the rope and put it back in the basket.

'I shan't go in for the skipping race,' she said loudly, 'because it's babyish.'

'I am,' said Christopher, 'and I'm going in for the sack race.'

'I'm going in for everything except skipping,' said Melanie Brown and she hurried away to practise the three-legged race with Denise. They stood side by side and Miss Bradley tied Melanie Brown's right leg to Denise's left leg. They were getting along quite well until Melanie Brown's plimsoll came off and she stopped so suddenly that poor Denise fell over. Denise was rather cross about that and said that she didn't want to be Melanie Brown's partner. Melanie Brown said she didn't care anyway and she untied the rope and gave her plimsoll a big kick which sent it flying across the field. It was such fun that Melanie Brown decided not to bother with any more practising, and she spent the rest of the afternoon kicking her plimsoll.

So by the time Sports Day arrived and all the mothers and fathers were coming to watch, Melanie Brown's name was down for only one race and that was the sack race. But Melanie Brown had never even been inside a sack and certainly hadn't practised racing in one. Christopher, however, had practised for hours in his back garden.

'I bet I win,' he said gleefully. 'I bet I win the prize.'

Melanie Brown's eyes opened wide with astonishment.

'Prize?' she said. 'Are there going to be prizes?'

'Of course,' said Christopher. 'First prize and second prize.'

Before she could ask what sort of prizes it was time for the first race. It was a running race and Denise and John were in it. They stood with the others on the special white line Mr Bloggs had painted on the grass.

'Ready – steady – go!' cried Mrs Jones, and all the mothers and fathers and the rest of the school started

shouting to encourage them.

'Go on, Denise! Go on!' shrieked Melanie Brown and she was so excited she couldn't stand still but had to jump up and down. Denise didn't quite win, but she was second, and came running back to show off her prize, which was a colouring book.

'You are lucky,' said Christopher. 'I wonder what I shall win.'

At last it was time for the sack race and each child

was given a sack. Melanie Brown's sack smelt dusty
and felt scratchy to her legs, but she put one foot into
each corner as she was told and held the top edge close
to her chest.

'Ready – steady – go!'

Melanie Brown took a great leap forward – and fell
over. She could hardly believe it. One minute she was
standing up and the next she was on the grass, all
muddled up in her sack. Ahead of her she could see
Christopher and the others leaping along as though it
were the easiest thing in the world.

'Get up, Melanie!' shouted Denise and Susan – and
John and Paula and Nicholas and Stephen and Michael
and a few more . . . 'Get up! . . . Melanie-e-e-e-e!'

Somehow she scrambled up and took another leap
forward. She wobbled – but she didn't fall over. She
took another leap – and another – and began to catch
up. Several of the others had fallen over and then two
bumped into each other and they fell over. Melanie
Brown went faster and faster and passed some of the
children who were slowing down a bit. Soon there was
only Christopher in front of her. He had almost
reached the winning line when he turned to see who
it was behind him – and *he* fell over! Melanie Brown
had won!

Everyone clapped, and Mrs Jones said, 'Well done,
dear,' and gave her the first prize, which was a small
pen with a golden tassel on the end of it. Christopher
got the second prize, which was a notebook.

'That's good,' said Melanie Brown, 'because we can
take turns with my pen to write in your notebook.'

Christopher thought it was good, too, so they found a shady corner under a big tree and left the rest of the school to finish Sports Day without them.

Melanie Brown and the Silver Horseshoe

Of course the children all knew that Miss Bradley was going to be married, but they didn't know when it was going to be. One day after Prayers the Head Mistress asked Miss Bradley to make a telephone call for her from the office.

'Now that Miss Bradley has gone,' she said to the children, 'we can talk about the secret. We are going to save up to buy a wedding present for Miss Bradley. If any of you would like to share in the present you can bring some money and Mrs Jones will collect it.'

Susan put her hand up.

'What is the present going to be?' she asked.

'We don't know yet,' said the Head Mistress. 'It might be a clock – or a table lamp – '

'Or a tin-opener,' said Melanie Brown. 'We gave my auntie a tin-opener when she got married and it goes on the wall and goes round and round by itself.'

'We'll think about it, Melanie,' said the Head Mistress, but then Miss Bradley came back into the hall, so they couldn't talk about it any more.

The children were very clever and Miss Bradley didn't guess that anything secret was going on. When they had collected all the money there was enough for a canteen of cutlery, and that is what they bought. All the children had a chance to see it before it was wrapped in the special wedding paper and gold ribbon. Even Melanie Brown had to admit that the knives, forks and spoons looked very beautiful on their bed of red velvet.

'Even better than a tin-opener,' she said generously.

The trouble came when one of the children had to be chosen to give the present to Miss Bradley. Melanie Brown was certain that they would choose her. But instead they chose Deborah, a girl in the top class, and Melanie Brown was very upset.

'It should b-be m-me,' she sobbed into her Horlicks, when her mother was putting her to bed that night. 'Miss Bradley l-loves me b-best, so why d-did they choose Deborah?'

Mrs Brown tried to explain that Miss Bradley was fond of all the children but they couldn't all give her the present. But Melanie Brown wouldn't be comforted. She cried and cried until her eyes were all red and her face was blotchy and Mrs Brown had to make her another cup of Horlicks to help her to go to sleep. Mrs Brown wondered what could be done to cheer her up again and she asked Grandmother.

'Why not let her give Miss Bradley a silver horseshoe?' said Grandmother, and it was such a good idea that Mrs Brown wished *she* had thought of it. Next morning was Saturday, so they went shopping and bought a silver horseshoe with a silver tape to hold it by. The horseshoe had 'Good Luck' written on it and Melanie Brown couldn't stop looking at it. She kept

opening the box to have another peep and she thought the day of the wedding would never come.

When it was time to give Miss Bradley the canteen of cutlery Deborah made a little speech and Miss Bradley made a little speech and everyone clapped and said, 'Three cheers for Miss Bradley.' Melanie Brown cheered louder than anyone else!

The wedding was at three o'clock on a Saturday, and most of the children and their mothers were there to see the bride and groom come out of the church. Miss Bradley looked very pretty in a long white dress and white veil. She carried a small bouquet of pink roses and a prayer book. The two little bridesmaids wore long dresses of primrose yellow and carried posies of white roses.

'I'm going to wear a dress like that when we're married,' Melanie Brown whispered to Christopher and she thought he looked pleased. A little surprised, maybe, but pleased.

When the bride and groom came out of the church after the service the photographer was waiting for them with a camera on a tripod. He arranged them in a neat group with the best man and the two brides-maids, then stepped back to adjust his camera.

'Give her the horseshoe now,' said Christopher. 'Go on!' But Melanie Brown had suddenly gone shy, so Christopher had to give her a push. Unfortunately he pushed her a bit too hard and she rushed forward at great speed and crashed into one of the bridesmaids. Both girls fell over on to the dusty path and the brides-maid's posy flew out of her hand into a clump of stinging nettles behind one of the gravestones. There was a great commotion. The bridesmaid cried and had to be comforted and the best man stung himself on the nettles when he retrieved the posy.

Melanie Brown sat on the path and explained in a loud voice that it was no good blaming her, because Christopher had pushed her. When she stood up again she discovered that she had been sitting on the horse-shoe. It was badly bent and would never be quite the same again.

The bride laughed so much that she cried and her make-up went a bit funny but finally everything was put right and they were ready for the photographs. Melanie Brown gave the horseshoe to Miss Bradley – who was now Mrs Collins – and she said she would keep it always. Mr Collins suggested that Melanie Brown should be in one of the photographs, because he didn't want to forget her – even if he could! Melanie Brown thought it was very nice of him and she stood next to him and held his hand.

The photograph was a good one and Melanie Brown keeps it on her window-sill between a satin pincushion and a china rabbit.

Melanie Brown and the New Class

One day Mrs Collins called six of the children together and told them that because they were so clever they could soon go up into the next class with Mrs Jones. Melanie Brown was one of the six and she listened carefully to what Mrs Collins had to say. Then she thought the matter over and decided against it.

'Because I like it best in this class,' she said. Christopher stared at her in horror.

'But I'm going,' he said. 'What will you do without me?'

Melanie Brown didn't know and she didn't care.

'I don't like Mrs Jones,' she said. 'She's not pretty – and she's a bit old.'

'She's not old,' said Denise, 'and she's ever so kind – and you do hard sums in her class.'

'That's true,' said Mrs Collins quickly. 'The work in this class is very easy really and you six are clever enough to do more grown-up work.'

'I like easy work,' said Melanie Brown firmly, and she went back to her table to finish her painting. Christopher's big blue eyes filled with tears as he looked at Mrs Collins.

'If Melanie's not going then I don't want to go,' he

said shakily.

'Nor do I,' said Paula.

John and Susan didn't say anything but they didn't look very happy. Mrs Collins sighed.

'Well,' she said, 'go back to what you were doing and we'll talk about it another day.'

'When I've sorted out Melanie Brown,' she added to herself and wondered how to go about it.

Melanie Brown was very pleased with her painting. It was a picture of a garden. She had put hundreds and hundreds of blades of grass at the bottom of the picture and big splodgy roses up each side. The middle was full of navy blue flowers. 'Primroses,' she told Paula, who looked rather surprised. She decided to add a big yellow sun and dipped her brush into the yellow paint. She drew a big round circle – and then gave a sudden roar of rage that shocked the whole class into silence.

'Melanie!' cried Mrs Collins. 'Whatever is the matter?'

'My picture!' shrieked Melanie Brown. 'It's all gone horrible! The sun's all green!'

They all crowded round and sure enough the sun was green. Not very green, it's true, but a nasty yellowy green, not a bit like the sun. Melanie Brown glared fiercely around, then pointed accusingly at the jar of yellow paint.

'Someone's mixed the colours,' she said. 'Someone's put the blue brush in the yellow.'

'Poor Melanie,' said Mrs Collins. 'What a shame. It was such a nice picture, too. Still, I'm sure it was an accident.'

'It was Michael,' said Denise. 'I saw him.'

Melanie Brown gave Michael a horrid look, snatch-ed her painting from the easel and screwed it up. She threw it on to the floor and started to cry. Christopher tried to cheer her up but in the end she had to sit on Mrs Collins's lap for a few minutes with a handful of Dolly Mixtures.

'Don't be cross with Michael,' said Mrs Collins. 'He is only five and he hasn't been at school long. He doesn't know about paints yet.'

Melanie Brown said nothing, but she sniffed very loudly several times and put five Dolly Mixtures into her mouth at once. Mrs Collins gave her a paper tissue to wipe her eyes with and suggested that she start another picture, but Melanie Brown had gone off the idea of painting and decided to read a book instead.

In the afternoon Mrs Collins asked Melanie Brown to take a note to Mrs Jones, and that pleased her, because she loved doing important things. She marched round to Mrs Jones's room and knocked on the door. The children called out, 'Come in,' so she did. She gave Mrs Jones the note and waited while she read it in case there was going to be an answer.

'Mrs Collins wants to borrow some books,' said Mrs Jones. 'While I'm finding them perhaps you would like to have a look round and see what the children are doing.'

So Melanie Brown began a tour of the room. In one corner she found some children mixing cake-mixture in a big bowl.

'We're making cakes,' they told her proudly. 'The cook is going to bake them in her big oven for us.'

In the Book Corner two boys were reading about aeroplanes and writing things down in their books. But it was the painting that interested Melanie Brown most. To her surprise there were no pots of paint like the ones they used in her own class. Instead the children had a small tray each. Six plastic pots fitted into each tray and these were filled with different-coloured powders.

'It's powder paint,' one of the boys told her kindly. 'We mix our own colours in this class. Look, I'll show you.'

He stirred some yellow and some red paint together and added a little water.

'There you are! Orange!'

Melanie Brown was enchanted.

'I know about mixing colours,' she said. 'I'll mix you some green.'

And before he could say, 'No thank you,' she had taken the brush and was mixing blue and yellow powder to make green.

'There you are,' she said proudly. 'Now you can have some grass in the picture.'

The boy was just explaining that it was a picture of a jet plane flying in the sky and he didn't need any grass, and Melanie Brown was telling him that a jet plane landing on some grass would be a much better picture, when Mrs Jones interrupted them.

'Here you are, Melanie,' she said. 'These are the books Mrs Collins wants to borrow and thank you for bringing the message.'

Reluctantly Melanie Brown went back to her own room. She put the books on Mrs Collins's desk without a word and stood deep in thought, scuffing the toe of one shoe along the floor. The teacher watched her hopefully. At last Melanie Brown gave a little sigh and looked up.

'I think I will go into Mrs Jones's class after all,' she said. 'She's not as old as I thought – and she is a *bit* pretty.'

Mrs Collins smiled broadly and said she thought Melanie Brown had made a very wise decision.